The Scots and the
Sassenachs

THE BARON'S
SAVING GRACE

RAVEN MCALLAN &
CASSIE O'BRIEN

The Baron's Saving Grace
ISBN # 978-1-80250-948-9
©Copyright Raven McAllan & Cassie O'Brien 2022
Cover Art by Fiona Jayde ©Copyright May 2022
Interior text design by Claire Siemaszkiewicz
Totally Bound Publishing

THE BARON'S
SAVING GRACE

Dedication

To Emmy Ellis, with love from us both.

Chapter One

The inn was well presented, had a good menu and served excellent ale. To say nothing of providing a supply of whisky he was certain had never been within scent of an exciseman.

George Armstrong, who following the death of his father now bore the title Baron Hexham, winced at the squawk the feet of his chair made as he pushed it back a few inches to allow him to cross one knee over the other and not upturn the nearby table. He sniffed the spirit in his glass, savoured the peaty aroma with appreciation and took a sip.

"Douglas, 'tis as good as ever," he said to the anxiously awaiting landlord. "You are a genius in securing something so special. What I wouldn't do for a cask of this at home." He laughed at the landlord's agonised expression. "No, I will not ask you to facilitate that. I imagine it is fraught enough getting sufficient for your needs."

"That it is, indeed, my lord. But if you wish I…"

George took pity on the man. He had been only half-serious when he'd said he wished he had some at home. It would have put the noses out of joint of the people who worked on his estate and had their own stills secreted away. They may lie south of the border, but their appreciation—and copying—of the water of life was alive and kicking. He had no idea where they secreted the still whose results he regularly acquired, but he hoped it was never discovered by the powers that be. The resultant whisky was as good as the one he now savoured. "Do not worry yourself. It's another good reason to visit you. Along with your wife's cooking and a comfortable bed on my journey."

"That's grand. May I ask how t'house is comin' on?"

George sighed. His Corbridge home had been razed to the ground by his laudanum-addicted father, and his addlepated sire had perished in the blaze. "Slowly, Douglas, very slowly. The one redemption from the whole sorry state is no one but the late baron was hurt when he ventured too near the flames." He chose not to mention the man had been as naked as a jay and waving a bottle of port, *or* that he could never forgive himself for not remembering that whilst under the influence Gordon, his late father, had been irrational and likely to fall into a rage. The conflagration had been because George had foiled his parent's plans to ruin a man whose long-dead ancestor, his father had believed, had caused a curse to be laid upon the Armstrong family. In his drug-clouded mind, Gordon had invented a ruinous theory of the curse being broken by way of a marriage between the two families, and had stooped to the lowest form of blackmail to bring this about. That was the manner of man he had been. George hoped and prayed he had none of the man's unpleasant traits in him. "He thought he saw someone

8

or something inside." A lie, but who was to confront him over it?

"Ah, good man, sorry ending." The landlord shook his head in sorrow. "Life must go on though, eh? You off north?" Douglas' voice penetrated George's mind, and he brought himself back to the present.

George nodded. "To the Trossachs, to see a good friend who lives there. Then I'm away to the Tay for the fishing before the season ends."

"Then I'll wish ye well," Douglas replied. "I'd not be wantin' to go so far m'sen but I know you gentry folk are happy wi' all t'travel. Will you be using the private parlour later this evening?"

Amused at the idea that only those higher up the social ladder travelled, George blinked at the change of topic and considered the question, while pondering the types of people who also travelled. What about salesmen? Servants changing jobs? Drovers, herders and itinerants? The list could be endless. He mentally laughed at himself and let the thoughts go.

As to his present abode, he was comfortable where he was. The room was aptly named the snug. Three tables, two benches and four high-backed armchairs with padded seats. Set in front of a crackling fire with a bell pull for service. What more could he want? Except for a warm and willing body and that was as unlikely as a Stuart returning to the throne. "Not if you need it for someone else. I'll be as happy here."

"Then I'll tell the gentleman who wishes to use it with his ward that he may." The landlord sounded relieved. "The lass has had a touch of nausea after travelling, so they're biding the night. Last two rooms, they got. We're mighty busy this day. The sheep sales, you know."

George nodded. Not that he did know a lot, but he'd intended to take a look at the sales and see if anything there interested him. His estate in the Cheviots would stand a few additions to the flock and Callum, his shepherd, was due the following day to look the animals over. They'd been told some of a flock with outstanding pedigrees would be up for auction. A couple of rams and an ewe or two wouldn't go amiss.

George would leave everything to Callum, hand him the cash they had decided on and keep well away. Callum was an unknown in the area — George himself was not. He wouldn't put it past some farmers to collaborate to push the prices up if it were known he was bidding. His father hadn't shown their family in a good light in the area. George accepted he would have an uphill struggle to rectify it.

He settled down in front of the fire, legs crossed at the ankle, and steepled his hands on his chin. Deep in thought, he studied the flames for a while and pondered on how fire could be both good — here at that moment — and bad — the way his home had ended up as ashes.

With another dram and several of the landlady's famed-throughout-the-area singing hinnies, he contemplated all he needed to do in the next few weeks. Singing hinnies, sweet griddle cakes, which George, along with a large percentage of the local population, were partial to, were a local favourite, and everyone guarded their own specific recipe jealously.

George's mind moved from the future to the past as he mused over the previous twelve months. They had been frenetic, worrying and, thankfully at times, uplifting. With the exception of the fire and the tragedy of his father's death, there had been more positives than negatives, and at last George felt his life was on an even keel.

Apart, of course, from his still being unwed. Not something that had overly bothered him in the past, but now seeing new — but good — friends happily settled, he was aware he thought he would like a wife. Children. A family. An heir.

How he was to achieve that he had no idea. A season paying court to the well-brought-up young ladies on the marriage mart held little appeal — even if he'd been so inclined. His father's antics, plus his own once well-deserved but no longer relevant reputation as a rake, would ensure no parent worth their salt would consider him a good bet as a husband for their daughter.

He sighed and stared into his tankard of ale as if it had all the answers.

It didn't. He took one mouthful, twisted the tankard around and watched the contents froth. How long before it fell flat? A bit like he felt at that moment.

George was not the sort of person to think every solution was found in the bottom of a jug of ale or a flagon of whisky, and had no idea how long it was before he became aware of voices from the adjoining room. Seconds probably. He put his drink down and debated whether to scrape his chair over the floor to show the occupants the private parlour, it seemed, wasn't exactly private.

Whether it was due to the way the chimneys met and merged or doors ajar he had no idea, but two voices could be clearly heard.

"I told you I'll come with you and marry you, so why all this farridaddle?" a female voice asked. "If you don't think I'll be true to my word, lock me in my room. Try to make me share yours, and I'll bring the roof down and cause such a scandal you won't have a hope of your plot succeeding. Your choice."

"You better be on the level."

George decided not to announce his presence and narrowed his eyes, as if by doing so he could see though walls or even identify the speaker. Did he know him? He certainly had never heard the female voice before, but the deeper baritone sounded familiar.

"I am as on the level as you are," the lady — he was certain she *was* a lady, a gently reared female — continued. "I would do nothing to harm my family, even if you are not so scrupulous. I will not let any scandal stick to Papa or the memory of my late mama, and you know that fine well. Otherwise, you wouldn't have thought up this insidious plan. One, I might add, only a scoundrel would choose to carry out. Now, kindly go and locate the landlord and discover which room I have been allocated so I may retire for the evening. *Alone.*"

For a few seconds there was silence, then the male answered.

"Very well. Wait here. But remember..." The tone George supposed was meant to be menacing had more than a hint of a whine in it. And *now* he recognised it.

Adrian Corbett, by God. The blaggard! What is he up to?

"Oh, I remember it all. You can be sure I will go to my room, but do not think to accompany me to it, because if you do, I will..." There was a pregnant pause. "Create. A. Scene."

George mentally applauded the lady. Not many well-bred females of his admittedly limited acquaintance would have the sense — or temerity — to act in such an assertive way.

A door creaked open and footsteps sounded on the wooden boards of the hallway outside the snug.

12

George considered not just the words he'd overheard but also the disdain and loathing in the female's voice. Whoever the lady may be, she was obviously being coerced into a marriage against her natural inclination. She had sounded feistily determined to stand her ground, but would her words be enough to hold a man like Adrian Corbett at bay should he decide to enter her room after imbibing a couple of brandies?

The thought turned George's stomach. The man was certainly foul enough to physically force his presence on a slighter-built female. He would probably excuse himself doing so without a second thought if she was destined to be his wife. It was not to be borne. No female should be forced into marriage. With anyone. George set his glass on the table, walked quickly to the door and left the room.

* * * *

Grace Foston stared at the back of the parlour door as it shut behind the detestable Adrian Corbett and discovered she was breathing heavily, almost as if she had been out for a long hard gallop on her favourite pony then swum in the river. Both things which were frowned upon in the circles she moved in.

The bloody man. The gall *and*, she allowed, the cleverness he showed. Her poor, poor sister.

In Corbett's absence she retied and tightened the ribbons of the poke bonnet she had selected that morning for the fact of it having a large-rounded brim that shaded the top half of her face. And just in time. For not two minutes after her nemesis departed, the door handle turned again. The landlord must have been hovering nearby. However, to her surprise, it was not Corbett who entered the parlour but a man she had never seen before in her life. He beckoned her towards him then held out his hand.

"Come. Quick. Before he returns."

This not being part of Grace's master plan in the slightest, she stood but moved no closer. "Ah…this is a private parlour, sir. I request you leave it."

The man's tone became more urgent as he walked towards her. "No. No. I won't have it. Especially not with him."

Grace glared and opened her mouth to object, but before she could speak, found herself captured in a bear hug and lifted from her feet.

"Forgive me, but I cannot allow you to stay here with such a man."

Held in an embrace so tight there was no room to so much as wriggle, Grace couldn't find enough breath to scream.

What could she do?

The handle of the furled parasol she'd hung on the back of her chair brushed against her hand as he began to walk toward the door. She curled her fingers around its ivory shaft and managed to take it with her as she was carried unceremoniously from the parlour and up the stairs to her abductor's room.

Each firm footstep echoed in her mind. Like the steps to doom.

Stop being fanciful, she chided herself. *Doom is not allowed in this establishment, or in my foreseeable future.* She hoped.

The man set her back on her feet and released her after toeing the door shut behind them. Grace seized her chance and set about him with her silk-covered sunshade. He yelped at the first blow. The whalebone shaft shattered at the second, and the delicate ivory sticks of its ribs disintegrated as she pummelled his arms. He held his hands up to protect his head from further assault.

"Damnation, woman. Stop it, you hellcat. I'm saving you from a fate worse than death here. Ow! That hurt. Why did I even bother…?"

His words gave Grace pause. She surveyed the mangled parasol and dropped it with a thud. It would never be the same. "Now look what you've made me do. It's ruined. Who are you and what on earth made you step forward as you did?" She glanced around for something near at hand that could also be used as a weapon. Two vases and a heavy, ugly statue of a naked nymph could be easily reached. Reassured, she stared at the man. "I demand an explanation at once." She stamped her foot. "And I meant it, or else." *What a stupid statement. Or else what?* "Explanation. Now."

She was not at all certain she'd get one. Handsome, engaging and no doubt a rake, he wouldn't be the sort of person to tamely reply. He had the look about him — that of a man who would do as he preferred and not kowtow to conformity.

The intruder rubbed his head, where she could see a lump was already forming. He smiled, ruefully. "George Armstrong. At your service, and to rescue you from the clutches of a man no sane person would spend a minute with. Otherwise, it won't only be the parasol that is ruined." He held out his hand. "If you wish to escape him, come with me now. We don't have a lot of time."

She ignored his offer and resolutely tamped down the hint of sympathy for the injury she had bestowed on him. He deserved it. His face might be unfamiliar, but his name was not. The antics of a certain Mr G A of Corbridge had made regular appearances in the scandal sheets over the years. Why on earth hadn't she kept her pistol in her reticule instead of stowing it in her portmanteau? She glanced towards the most substantial vase in the room. She would have no chance to reach it before he overpowered her. The nymph it would have to be. She had an irrelevant thought of the statue's prominent breasts hitting him in a place he would find *very* painful.

"George Armstrong… I've heard of you."

He flinched as if the note of disgust in her voice had administered a direct slap to his face. Why? Gossip might be unreliable but there would not have been quite so much of it in the press unless there was some element of truth in the loose behaviour they accused him of.

"I should have hit you harder," Grace said forcefully. "As it is, my poor parasol will never be opened again. Who are you to tell how me how to go on? You…you…rake…" She didn't add she had also heard of his prowess as a lover, although being face to face with his broad shoulders and undoubted good looks, she had no trouble believing the truthfulness of those particular rumours. Not that she intended to let them influence her. Not at all. So why were her nerve ends tingling? Why were her palms clammy and her mind sending amorous thoughts to her brain? Along the lines of 'wouldn't it be good to find out'?

Enough. Concentrate on the necessities of this situation.

His mouth quirked up at the corners and a twinkle entered his blue eyes, as if what she had just said amused him.

"A rake?" he drawled, in the best rakish voice she had heard in an age. "I'm not sure I'd go so far as to call myself that, not these days at any rate, although I will admit to the odd peccadillo or several in my past. Due to those, ah…interesting times, and given my youthful follies, I have experience of how a rake's mind works. I've met many a man like Corbett. I hope not to meet many more, but I don't hold my breath. They seem to go forth and multiply at a formidable rate."

Grace looked longingly at the nymph once again then glared at him. *Youthful follies? Not if the papers are to be believed. Is he addled?*

"Are you an aficionado of the poppy, Mr Armstrong?" It was the most scathing thing she could think of on the spur of the moment.

Any hint of humour fled from his face. He reddened.

Maybe that was a bit too much. He appears ready to commit murder. Probably mine. Grace opened her mouth to apologise, but before she had a chance to speak, he beat her to it.

"I am not," he replied stiffly. "I have no need of such things, be they medicinal or not. As for Corbett, I have no clue as to whether he has any unsavoury addictions, although I do know he's a less-than-honourable man. A weasel. A reprobate of the first order. An underhanded rogue." He raised his shoulders and let them fall. "Count your fingers after he has held your hand. He's the type of person whose only consideration is for himself and what is best for him. Nothing else. Why on earth is someone like *you* here with someone like *him*?" His voice was desolate, and his bleak expression made her wince.

However, she was wise enough to know any sympathy would not, at that given moment, be well received. Grace held her tongue, striving not to let her temper get the better of her and fairly sure she would not succeed. After all, what did he know?

Given his father's sad history, the lady's question had stung, although she would not realise why it had caused him pain. Her next words had him within an inch of showing her the door and leaving her to fend for herself, but he could not bring himself to do it. No female should be left in Corbett's clutches, let alone one as tempting as the apple-cheeked beauty stood in front of him now.

"This is folly," he said in what he hoped was a reasonable tone, and suspected she would disagree. "Someone needs to tell you."

She pursed the perfect bow of her lips. "So you say."

She disagreed. God save me from a bloody contrary woman. Even if she does make my body tighten and my cock stretch my breeches.

"As I've told you. I know so."

And if you believe different you deserve all you get.

"Your opinion, sir, is nothing I need to have regard for." She clenched her fists.

George watched her warily. Women could be unpredictable and he knew to his cost this one had a strong arm and could use it to great success. It would be preferable if she didn't have cause to use it in his direction in the future.

"I am damned sure you do, woman. I rescued you."

The lady sent a glowering glance in his direction. One silk-slipper shod foot beat a soft but determined staccato rhythm on the carpeted floor.

"Do not call me woman in that tone, *sir*."

How had she made 'sir' sound a like an epithet?

"I didn't need rescuing," the lady went on in the same 'explaining to a simpleton' tone. "My sister and I are similar enough in looks for me to fool Corbett into thinking I am her. Especially when aided by a large-brimmed bonnet and a parasol to hide the fact that my eyes are green rather than blue and my hair is lighter in colour than hers."

George couldn't help himself and grinned. She sounded interesting and took his mind away from his problems. "Why on earth would you need to do that?"

She eyed him in a considering way, as if making up her mind about him. Did she think him untrustworthy?

"For my ears only," he added. "I might appear someone who shares, but trust me I do not." He chuckled. "No rake or rogue worth their salt would gossip, and no ex-rake doubly so."

Then she nodded, plonked herself down on the padded boudoir chair with a sigh and removed her headgear. She tossed it onto the floor and pressed her fingers to her temples as if to massage away pain. Should he ask if she had a headache? Perhaps not. She might say yes and that he was the one who had caused it.

"Ahh, that's better. Let me try and explain. Around seven years ago, Mama passed away in tragic circumstances—she slipped and fell into the river Freshney, which was swollen with winter rains, caught pneumonia and died within days. Not long after, Papa remarried. He's one of those men who need to have a wife." She twisted her lips. "I've never been sure why. After all, half the time he's not at home. Which is by the by. My sister, Jane, still resides at the family home, and our stepmother resents this. She wants her gone. We don't know the reason, for her attitude, except perhaps it interferes with her social life." Grace paused and smiled wryly. "Including the...ah...how should I put it..."

"Shenanigans? Peccadillos?" George nodded. "It happens."

"Sadly. As you say. My poor papa. To make matters worse, you will find Corbett's name on my stepmother's family tree, albeit on a different branch.

Jane and I believe if she is not actually in cahoots with Corbett, she has encouraged and aided his pretentions to Jane's hand."

George pulled the high-backed chair from the desk and sat on it. "Why? Is Jane a great heiress or something?"

The lady's smile, although rueful, lit her face and nearly took George's breath away. "No. We each have a small dowry along with a few hundred pounds inherited from Mama to be given to us on the day we marry. Corbett's obsession with Jane is purely lust, I fear."

If the sister was in anyway comparable with the lady sat opposite him, George could see why Corbett desired her. Another's encouragement coupled with the man's own shady morals clarified for him how the situation had come to be. Apart from one point. "Ah… So two sisters alike in looks and circumstances. What makes you an unacceptable alternative to Jane?"

"Alike in looks? Enough, unless we are stood side by side, but I reside in Harrogate and Jane in Knaresborough, so Corbett has never seen me in person and it does not naturally occur to him that Jane is not Jane. A few theatricals on my part have kept him on his toes and his mind rather too busy to think it through. Alike in circumstances? Not at all. Jane is unwed because she has been waiting for the man she loves to return from active duty. When she got wind of what Corbett was plotting, she appealed to the colonel of his regiment, who luckily is a distant relative to our late mama. The upshot being Major Winterbottom has been granted a period of compassionate leave. If my delaying tactics work according to plan, they will arrive at Gretna ahead of myself and Corbett. When we ourselves get there, Corbett will discover Jane is now married, and he is in the company of the wrong sis…"

Her words trailed off at the sound of a tap on the door. It opened and the landlord walked into the room, his arms full of logs for the fire. Douglas' eyes widened as surveyed George's female companion, and his face reddened. "Um… Please accept apologies, my lord. I didn't realise you had…ah…company."

He deposited the logs in a wicker basket beside the grate, lit the oil lamps on the mantel with a taper flamed in the fire and backed hastily out of the room.

That's done it! There's only one honourable way out of this.

George opened his mouth to speak the words and found they came easily, as if this were his destiny. The way it was always meant to be. "Would you do me the great honour of becoming my wife?" He waited for her answer with bated breath.

Her face softened. "How very kind of you, but I'm afraid my answer must be no. Perhaps by way of an explanation I could offer you my name?"

George's heart sank. He nodded as his mouth went dry. He suspected he was in for an unpleasant surprise.

"The Honourable Mrs Roger Foston."

His assumption had been correct.

Mrs? Roger Foston? But he's even older than my father would be now…

Whatever else he had expected to hear, it was not this. Eloquence fled. Instead of a polite 'pleased to meet you', only two words escaped his mouth. "How? Why?"

He received an amused smile accompanied by a shrug. "How? Well, in the normal manner. Roger proposed, and I accepted. We were wed in the local church a few weeks later. Why? Well, there are worse situations to find oneself in than to be wed to a good-natured man who treats his wife with respect and understands not all women are without a brain, and that some need more from life than an endless round of parties and tittle-tattle."

In the face of her refreshingly candid reply, George gathered his scattered wits and walked to a long side table. The contents of the decanters standing on it he had investigated earlier, before descending the stairs to spend the evening in the snug. He poured a glass of ratafia for her and a large tot of whisky for himself. "More than residing in a home where you are neither welcome nor wanted, for instance?"

"Amongst other things." She took the wine from him, had a sip and made a face before she put the glass down on a nearby table. "Good grief, it is revoltingly sweet. What are *you* drinking?"

He handed her his glass with a bow, fully expecting her to decline. She didn't. Instead, she lifted it to her nose, sniffed the contents and smiled in appreciation before she tasted.

"Ah, Glen Eyevie, I suspect. Good choice. I do wonder how on earth it arrived here? Old Angus McSporran is very careful whom he selects to be a recipient of his talents, and his very words I believe are he *'cannae stand most o' thon sassenachs'*." She laughed. "You appear surprised I know such things? My husband is happy to introduce me to such niceties as a good malt. We may be sassenachs, but we both have ancestors from north of the border."

He nodded but made no comment regarding her or her husband's antecedents, instead content to keep things harmonious and to the point.

"A fine whisky for a fine lady." He poured himself a fresh measure. "*Slàinte.* Your husband is obviously a man of discerning taste, Mrs Foston." He hoped she didn't understand the underlying implications in his words, or if she did, she accepted his admiration without reservation.

She put the glass down and held out her hand. "Being as I'm in your bedroom, albeit unwillingly, you'd best call me Grace."

George shook it gently and managed the words he hadn't been capable of earlier. "Pleased to meet you, Grace, and please accept my apologies. My actions were ill-conceived but not ill-intentioned."

A challenging glint entered her eyes. "Ill-conceived, certainly. Ill-intentioned? I have yet to make up my mind. Do you make a habit of forcibly removing females according to your own summation of their situation?"

George picked up the gauntlet and ran with it. "About as often you adopt a false persona purposefully to deceive, I suspect."

His remark hit home. Grace's face flushed.

Chapter Two

Well, really. The cheek of the man. She'd been a fair way to liking George Armstrong up until then. However, his words held a hint of truth, and her face heated even more as she glared at him and voiced her objection. "I beg your pardon? Are you accusing me of being a fraud?"

He crossed one elegantly clad leg over the other and sat back more comfortably in his chair. Sadly, the position highlighted every line of his body, including his interesting — and it appeared interested — manhood. She averted her eyes and willed her pulse to slow down. He might be a fine specimen but he was not hers, nor could he be. The short, sharp shock of disappointment surprised her. No man had provoked such a reaction from her in an age.

"Oh, don't poker up so," he said in an amused voice. "I was merely pointing out that for the best of reasons each of us has stepped outside the boundaries acceptable to our status in our endeavours to provide assistance to another person."

George's stance was relaxed, his voice mild, and her ire faded. He had a point. "Yes. Well. I suppose so."

A smile lit his handsome face. "That's better, even if I suspect it was dragged out of you. You're here with your husband's approval then? He knows of your plan?"

The tug of attraction tightened in Grace's stomach then made itself known in her nether regions. *Oh, God. He is a charmer.* Unsettled by her body's instantaneous response, Grace pressed her knees together and refocused on the matter in hand. "Yes and no. Roger and I agreed I should go post-haste to Jane's assistance, but I didn't confide the finer details of how I planned to solve her dilemma. These days, my husband is in poor health." She closed her eyes for a brief second to hide the sadness she felt for Roger. Very much older than her but considered 'young for his years' at the time of their courtship, his health had taken a sudden turn for the worse within a year of their marriage. "Roger's heart is not as it should be. His physician says he is as comfortable as I can make him and he is content to live quietly in our Yorkshire home, watch the sea in all its moods and take an interest in the affairs of the village." She sighed. "I would never have left him if my sister hadn't been in such dire straits, but his valet is devoted, and Jane's need was greater, so..."

"I'm sorry. I didn't realise his health was failing."

"You are acquainted with him, I believe? He has mentioned your name from knowing you in earlier years when he himself was in better health."

George frowned. "Ah... Are you sure it is me you have heard about? I have no recall of having ever met your husband."

"Baron Armstrong?"

He nodded. "That is me."

"Then of course I am sure. Your exploits are legendary."

"But was it George or Gordon? I admit I had my moments before maturity, but I am no compatriot of your husband. He is of an age comparable to my late father. I believe they may have been acquaintances. Probably through being members of some of the same clubs."

A sinking feeling hinted she might have made a terrible mistake in thinking the worst of his reputation. "I only know 'G'. Are you telling me that is not you?" She almost added, 'it appears to be somewhat far-fetched for it not to be', however some niggle in the back of her mind made her bite her tongue.

"I'm George. My father was Gordon. I had my day, but I couldn't compare my youthful exploits to those of the previous generation." He smiled wryly. "They went at their hedonistic pleasures with no thought for anyone else. I, at least, took care not to hurt or embarrass those who were innocent."

Thank goodness she hadn't expanded on her earlier statements and shredded his character completely. Grace felt faint at the thought of what unpleasantness her misconception could have caused. She made haste to explain herself further.

"Thank you for clarifying your situation." She glanced at the clock and jumped. "Now what do we do? Corbett will be searching for me. If the landlord recognised me from being with him earlier, the game will be up. I still need to keep him away from Gretna until at least the day after tomorrow. By my reckoning, Jane will now have left the church after marrying her beloved major. This night was to be their wedding night so they can..." Heat rushed into her cheeks.

Those details shouldn't be shared with an almost stranger.

"Consummate their marriage?" George suggested without any inflexion.

"As you say," she said, grateful for his mild explanation. Why hadn't she thought of it? "Then when Corbett and I arrived at Gretna, she and her husband were to get me out of his clutches, by force if necessary." She took a deep breath. "Do you follow all I've said?"

George nodded with appreciation. "Oh yes, and I must add, if you were to use your parasol on Corbett to the same effect as you did on me, their interference would not be needed."

She grinned. "I had hoped so." She sobered. "What now?"

George thought quickly. A well-deserved uppercut to the jaw administered with pleasure by himself would render Corbett unconscious. A couple of days confined to the landlord's cellar should suffice for him to be able escort Grace to meet her sister at Gretna unaccosted. He knew the innkeeper well enough to be confident Douglas would oblige, but before he could recommend this course of action to his guest, a noisy kerfuffle sounded outside in the hallway—a recognisably unwelcome voice shouting something about a missing person, for which heads would roll. His door shook and rattled under the stress of several hard thumps.

"Hoy, you in there, open up." Corbett's voice was full of fury. "My ward has been seen in your company. I demand to search your room."

"Sir, you cannot... I implore you..." That was the landlord. "You will disturb my other patrons."

The hammering increased in noise and intensity. The door wasn't locked – a fact George guessed would not remain long undiscovered, given the ferocity of the blows. Grace cursed softly and jumped to her feet. "Damn. This not the moment for him to discover I'm not Jane. It's too soon."

She reached for her bonnet. George expected her to put it on but instead she thrust it toward him and hissed, "When he forces his way in here, it'll be simpler all round if he finds you alone. Hide this under the bed and stow what remains of my parasol with it." Then she darted to the window and threw up the sash.

"W-what? Wait. You can't." George stuttered as he realised her intention.

Grace raised her eyes heavenward to the starlit night sky and huffed. "Typical man. Just watch me." With a flash of a well-turned ankle, she climbed over the ledge and onto the overhanging branch of the tree outside it. Then, as nimbly as any young lad, she vanished into the depths of its dense summer foliage, out of sight.

George moved quickly, closing the window and hiding her bonnet and parasol as requested. The half-full glasses he secreted behind the taller bottles on the side table before striding to the door and opening it at the next thump.

Corbett fell in through the aperture and lost his footing as his impetus propelled him forward.

"To what do I owe this non-pleasure?" George enquired as Corbett, thanks to one end of his undone cravat having settled over his eye, peered myopically up at him from the floor. "I hope you have a good explanation."

"He said the last time he'd seen my ward she was talking to you." Corbett spat the words out. "Show me."

Standing in the doorway behind Corbett, the landlord appeared beside himself with worry. "I'm sorry, my lord. He didn't ask his question all open like that, and I spoke without thinking."

George gave Douglas a reassuring smile, and the man visibly relaxed, so he returned his attention to Corbett, who was struggling to his feet.

George fixed him with a pointed stare. "Your ward, you say? Are you sure? Do enlighten me as to the circumstances, because I'm having difficulty thinking of a single person who would be addlepated enough to saddle a ward with you."

Corbett reddened and scowled. "I'm not sure I appreciate your insinuations." He straightened his jacket to restore his appearance.

George directed his best 'who on earth do you think you are expression' towards the man, then stepped closer, pulled back his arm and planted a facer directly onto Corbett's jaw. "No. I don't suppose you do. No more than I appreciate your filthy lies, you blackguard."

Corbett's eyes rolled back in his head as he crumpled to the floor again this time dazed and non-vocal.

"Oh, a good hit, my lord," Douglas exclaimed admiringly. "I sensed he was a wrong 'un from the minute he arrived at the inn. Is the lady safe?"

George toed Corbett's recumbent form to ensure he was suitably comatose. "Yes, although you'll forgive me if I don't confide her story. It'll go easier for you if you don't know."

"Of course, my lord." Douglas nodded. "But if I can be of any further assistance, just ask."

George smiled. "Indeed, you can. The lady concerned requires escorting to join her newly married sister and this rogue needs to be kept somewhere secure to cool his heels for a couple of days while I do so. You have my word I have no unacceptable intentions. Not like this blackguard."

Douglas chuckled. "I have the very place. My root cellar has only way one in, no windows and, better still, is situated a suitable distance from the house so no-one will hear him if he kicks up a fuss."

George agreed. "Very good. At least he won't starve. Add a bucket of water to quench his thirst, and perhaps another for him to relieve himself?"

"Indeed, I will, and I'll also pour a bottle of brandy over him…" Douglas grinned. "Then when I go in search of some turnips two days hence, I'll swear the last time I saw him he was deep in his cups. Say he must have staggered off and entered the root cellar himself. Anyone seeing or smelling the state of him by the time he emerges will have no trouble swallowing my tale."

George squeezed Douglas' shoulder. "Good man. You take his top half. I'll take his feet. Let's get him safely stowed in the cellar before he comes round."

He reopened the window, half turned to Douglas and said loud enough for Grace to hear, wherever she had hidden, "That's him taken care of. Let's get going." He and Douglas lifted their burden and carried it to its temporary abode.

* * * *

When he returned to his room Grace was once more ensconced in her chair with two freshly poured glasses of whisky standing on the small table in front of her. "A nice uppercut, my lord. I nearly cheered, although I'm not sure whether your laying Corbett out cold has lessened my problems or added to them. Would you care to explain your reasoning?"

George grinned. "You saw it then? Through the window?"

"A perfect view. You might not have been able to see me, but with the room backlit by lamplight, I could see you."

George took a glass from the table and resumed his seat on the chair by the desk. "Douglas is a good man. He has promised to keep Corbett at bay for a couple of days while we make our way to Gretna."

She stiffened, her fingertips drumming a rhythmic tattoo on the tabletop. "*We*? I think I have already proved I am not some weakling of a female in need of constant male supervision. I am quite capable of making my own way to Gretna, thank you."

George's mouth twitched. *So feisty. What I wouldn't give to have a woman like Grace in my life...and bed. Mmmm...yes...bed. Naked, her hair tumbling down her back...* His groin twitched at the thought. He crossed his legs and dismissed the delightful picture from his mind. "I am sure you are," he said honestly. "However, like it or not I am now part of this escapade. I will not be left here to wonder as to its outcome. You can set out for Gretna on your own if you insist, but you will find me marching one step behind you every inch of the way regardless."

She eyed him appraisingly. "Very well, you may accompany me on the understanding you are neither saving nor rescuing me. You are a companion, no more."

"Agreed," George said quickly, before she could think on the matter any further and possibly change her mind. "Do we shake on it?"

Grace held out her hand, shook his and dropped it hurriedly, then picked up her glass and sipped. "So, I could see what was occurring in the room but not hear. How have you left matters?"

George toasted her and decided that when he was less occupied he would think over the short, sharp frisson he'd experienced as they'd touched. Now was not the time to indulge in such things. "The landlord knows no more than Corbett is a 'bad 'un' you need to get away from. I confided no other details. You were no longer in my room and Douglas has no clue as to where you disappeared to."

"Good. Let's keep it that way. I will hide here for the remainder of the night, and we will depart at first light," Grace said in a no-nonsense voice. "There is no moon and as I am sure you are aware the road is not safe during the hours of darkness. Not only from those who would seek to relieve an unwary traveller of their purse or worse, but potholes and bogs."

She really *was* determined to be in charge. George held back from commenting. She'd learn soon enough he intended to be an active participant regarding their journey. He couldn't help his gaze darting towards the bed, although that idea was shot down in flames by Grace immediately.

"I," she declared, "will be sleeping fully clothed on the bed. You will be spending the night in the armchair, covered by your greatcoat."

With an apologetic grin, George turned down the lamp wicks. "I didn't ask or assume. I just had a momentary lapse of politeness. Try to get some sleep, we will need our wits about us when we leave."

By the light of the fire Grace climbed onto the bed and pulled the coverlet over herself. "I intend to.

Goodnight." In the rosy glow she watched him loosen his cravat, settle back in the chair and extend his long legs. His head tipped to one side and found the comfort of the padded side wing. Grace smiled as his breathing became regular and even. In repose, she had leisure to study George without seeming rude, and he really was the most handsome of men.

What would it be like to bed a man who not only desires me, but for whom I also feel an equal passion for in return?

It certainly wasn't how it was with Roger. She was fond of him, very fond. He was so kind, and his courtship had been a soothing balm compared to the unpleasantness of living with a stepmother who detested both herself and Jane for no other than reason than she wanted to rule the roost and to have everyone, especially Papa, dance to her tune. Grace acknowledged she had been naive when she'd married, not knowing the difference between platonic love and one which also excited the senses. She hadn't been revolted by the physical union between husband and wife, but the passion had been sadly one-sided and since Roger's illness any intimate contact had ceased to exist at all. A loving friendship was what she and Roger had now, and in the main Grace was content with her life, but sometimes… She took a last look at George's sleeping form and with a small sigh turned her cheek to the pillow and shut her eyes.

* * * *

The cacophony of the dawn chorus woke her at daybreak. She yawned and sat up. George, still asleep, emitted a soft snuffle. Grace grinned, picked up her pillow and sent it flying in his direction. "Stir yourself, lazybones."

Her missile hit its mark with a soft *flump*. George stirred and opened one bleary eye. "Good grief, is that any way to greet a man in the morning?"

Grace laughed.

He sat straighter and rubbed his fingers over the morning bristles on his chin. "And so bright and breezy too. Lord, I could do with a wash and shave."

Grace glanced ruefully at her own crumpled, slept-in day clothes. "As could I. Well, not the shave obviously, but I don't have my portmanteau or even know where it is. You interrupted before I was informed as to which room I'd been allocated."

George stood and stretched. "I need speak to Douglas and say I need to hie home but will be back soon. I must leave coinage and a message for my shepherd, Callum, and let him know to do as he thinks fit at the sales. I best not enquire of your luggage. After all, we're not supposed to be acquainted, and although our landlord is reliably discreet, I can place no such trust in the staff he employs. I can arrange for a change of clothes for you though. My friend Duncan lives roughly on our route and has a wife who will come to our aid. We all helped one another through a crisis a while back, and their marrying was the only good consequence to come out of it." He grimaced. "That all the trouble was caused by my laudanum-addicted father they are kind enough to ignore in favour of insisting his actions led to their current happiness in the wedded state. They own a property not so far from here. I was due to visit them there after the sheep sales, before we all venture farther north to indulge in some country sports. If we make a short detour, Cairstine will supply all the essentials you need to travel on to Gretna in some degree of comfort."

Grace's cheeks heated a little. *Blast! Poppy aficionado? I really hit a sore spot there, then.*

They sounded such a tight-knit group she hesitated to intrude. "Will that not be putting them to rather too much trouble? It seems an imposition. They do not know me."

"No doubt they will say it's part of the debt we all owe to each other."

"And what do you call it?" she asked, intrigued and pleased to learn a little more about him.

"Friends who help each other out in times of need. How long before you are ready?"

Grace considered. All she needed was to use the facilities. Anything else could be achieved later. "If you leave me alone, five minutes."

"I will give you ten."

He was as good as his word. Grace did all she needed and tidied herself as best she could. She finger-combed her hair and rued the fact she had no brush or comb before she roughly plaited it and tied the ends together. It would do until she found some ribbon or string. When George tapped on the door, she felt able to bid him enter with equanimity.

Until she glanced at his face and saw his strained expression. "What?" she demanded. "What is wrong?"

He grimaced. "Corbett's so-called valet is dozing in the tap room with the door open. The snores are not authentic. The only other way out is somewhat congested as the landlord is having alterations made to the kitchens, and the staff will be stirring any minute. You should not be seen with me if it can be managed."

"The man's name is Snodgrass," Grace informed George. "Valet, coachman and all-round rat-faced weasel. Awful specimen of humanity. To avoid him had I best make use of the tree again?"

"Hmm…" George frowned. "It then poses a problem when you reach the ground. It's open viewing from there to where we get our horses."

"Horses, plural?"

"I've persuaded Douglas I require to hire an additional pack horse to carry a little extra baggage I've managed to pick up…"

"Baggage?" Grace grinned. "Well, it's a novel way of describing me, for sure."

George eyed her thoughtfully. "We have a short walk to get to where Douglas will have tethered them, but it is at least out of sight on the other side of the building. I wonder… As you are accomplished with climbing trees, how are you with ladders? Of the rope kind."

Grace couldn't help laughing. What had started out as a way of helping her sister to achieve her heart's desire was now becoming decidedly interesting. She was conscious she'd been feeling ever older before her time these last few months with the staid lifestyle she led, but this adventure was certainly reviving her spirits and her yearning for a little excitement. "I am reasonably proficient with all kinds of ladders, rope or otherwise. Well," she added honestly, "I was during my hoydenish girlhood, and although I have found no need of such skills in recent years, I hope I have not lost the art. Surely such a skill, once learned, is never forgotten?" She hoped. "Lead me to it." Grace wondered just where George would procure a rope ladder. It was not something he would routinely carry in his luggage, was it? The riddle was soon solved though.

"Splendid." George grinned. "When Douglas showed me the horse available for hire, I spied a rope ladder coiled in the corner of the stable. The lads must use it to access the hay loft. I will liberate it. I think it best if I follow my normal morning routine. My washing water will arrive shortly…" He looked pointedly at the wardrobe. "And you will apparently not be here."

She held her hands up in mock horror. "Outrageous, Mr. Armstrong. A tree, a rope ladder and now concealment within your bedroom furniture. Whatever shifts will you be putting me to next during the course of this adventure?"

"Well…" He smirked. "Conveniently located—just where we need it to be—is a communal dormitory where a bed may be hired for the night for those persons unable to afford a private room. Even more conveniently, beside it is an anteroom for said persons to perform their ablutions, which just happens to have a window overlooking the stable yard…"

"You wretch!" Grace spluttered. "The public dunny? What if said persons arrive to use the facilities and find me hiding in there?"

His grin widened. "It has a privacy bolt."

There was a knock on the door.

Grace lowered her voice to a muted mutter as she slipped silently inside the heavy mahogany wardrobe. "The night bucket had best not still be in situ." George's soft snort followed her in as she almost shut the door behind her, leaving a scant half an inch between door and jamb. The tiny aperture allowed in light and air, which was reassuring.

Through the gap she saw George casually put a small valise on the floor in front of her. Not close enough to block her exit but nearby—to make sure there was no need for anyone to approach her hiding place. George bid the newcomer to enter, and Grace heard the rustle of skirts and a gentle thud as something, presumably the jug of hot water, was placed on the dresser. A few pleasantries were exchanged, then the servant opened the bedroom door to leave the room, and she heard Snodgrass say clearly, "Anyone seen my master?"

She hoped George gave his answer of, "Not since yesterday. Why?" with a straight face. Grace knew she would have found it difficult to do so. George strode to the door and shut it with a distinct snap in the man's face.

Grace bided her time until she thought the coast should be clear then stepped out of her hiding place. George was standing in front of the washstand, its porcelain bowl filled with water from the ewer, the lower half of his face covered in soapy foam.

"All clear. Forgive me for subjecting you to my morning routine, but I can't appear at breakfast unshaved."

Grace knew men removed their bristles, but as the process was normally a private matter between a man and his valet, she had never seen it. She looked at the open cut-throat razor George held in his hand with interest. The honed silver blade glinted, dangerously sharp. One slip, and she was sure the implement would live up to its name. "Fascinating. You have to slide that over your face and neck every day, do you?"

He did so, leaving a wide ribbon of foam-free skin in the blade's wake. "Unfortunately, I do. Sometimes twice. I have a heavy beard, and look more like a ruffian than ever if I do not."

Grace peered closer. "Well, I'm surprised more men do not sport a beard then. I find being fastened into gowns and petticoats irksome but at least the activity does not come with such an element of danger."

"Most men will not attempt to barber themselves, but I prefer to travel light—in my own company—whenever possible, so made sure to practice the art before using the blade on myself."

Grace wondered just which brave soul had let him do so. "Good grief. On whom?"

George concentrated on his reflection in the mirror as he attended to the area between his nose and lips. "Not whom, but what. Large ripe tomatoes, until I could remove soap foam from them without damaging the skin."

She burst out laughing. "I'm glad to hear it. For my part, I was imagining a loyal but rather bloodied servant lurking somewhere in your past."

He smirked and patted his face dry with a soft cloth. "I am a man of many talents, you know. I can blacken and buff my own boots, dress and arrange my neckcloth, pack my bags and even saddle up, all without assistance."

"A very impressive list, Mr Armstrong. Arrange for someone to disappear?"

"Sadly not." He walked nearer, lifted her hand and pressed it to his cheek. "See, soft as a newborn babe."

His touch felt so intimate, Grace's heart missed a beat. Her fingers ached to stroke along his jawline, to trace the outline of his lips, and her knees turned to jelly. George gazed into her eyes and his expression softened. *Was he, could he be...similarly affected?*

The spell was broken at the sound of a door slamming shut in the distance. She pulled back her hand. He returned to the washstand, then with a few folds and twists added a cravat at the open neck of his shirt before shrugging on his jacket.

"I will check the hallway is clear."

He opened the door a crack then beckoned her forward. "Come. I'll show you where the public facilities are to be found."

Grace sped along behind him on silent feet, and they luckily encountered no one before they reached a door down the length of a corridor on the other side of the inn. She peered around the door and thanked the heavens when no malodorous odour attacked her nose. The night pot must have been taken to the cesspit and exchanged for a clean one.

"Lock it behind you. I will return as soon as I can and will whistle like this to prove it is me." He essayed a low, melodious, two-note sound.

Grace nodded and, once inside, slid the bolt home behind her.

Chapter Three

George walked downstairs, ostensibly to take breakfast, although in actuality to borrow the rope ladder. He mused over the effect Grace had on him whilst he did. Not in many years had he felt the pull of attraction so strongly. It was more than just a carnal desire to bed a beautiful woman, but rather a deep-rooted conviction that they belonged together like two sides of the same coin. He sighed at the hopelessness of it all, then pulled himself together and located the landlord in the taproom.

Several patrons were partaking of breakfast, so George gave him a cheery greeting for the benefit of those within earshot, like Snodgrass. "Good morning, Douglas. I find myself regrettably short of time this morning and must get on."

"Then I'll fetch your victuals —"

George stayed the man with a slight shake of his head. "Unfortunately, no, but I would appreciate a few minutes of your time if you can spare it."

Douglas nodded and came around to the customers' side of the wooden counter. George turned and led the way in the direction of the stables. Once they were away from prying ears, George took a small coin purse from his pocket. "I need to be away sharpish. Will you give this to my shepherd, Callum, when he arrives? With my message? We require at least one ram, and he can buy whatever stock of his choice with the remainder of the coins. He is then to walk them home in easy stages. I will inspect them when I myself return."

"That I will, my lord. May I offer you a paper wrap of bread and cheese for your travels? Perhaps with a corked flask of tea?"

George was pleased with the notion. He couldn't have contemplated eating breakfast whilst knowing Grace must also be hungry. This way they could both be fed. He patted the landlord's upper arm. "Good man. I accept and thank you. I'll pick it up once I've saddled my mount."

"Very good, my lord. The pack horse is in the stall beside your own."

A lone ostler was inside the stable barn, and George tossed him a coin to distract him. "Saddle them up, will you?"

"Fine 'oss that is, my lord," the ostler said in an admiring tone. "I'd know 'im anywhere, I would."

George smiled his thanks and caught a movement out of the corner of his eye. In the doorway, Snodgrass ducked out of sight, although not quite in time to pass unnoticed. George's stallion was a fine specimen with a blaze on its nose and one white forelock that made him stand out. There would be little chance of going unnoticed if he rode him. When Grace was in Cairstine's care refreshing her wardrobe, he would have a word with Duncan, he decided. Ask if he could stable Sampson with him and borrow a nondescript mount from his friend. With the ostler's attention engaged in his task, George strolled to the rope ladder neatly coiled beneath the hayloft then oh-so-casually removed his jacket, slid his forearm through the hemp loops and concealed them by laying his garment over his arm.

The back door to the barn was to his left, and he called over his shoulder as he slipped through it, "I'll return shortly with my luggage."

Having nearly been caught out by Snodgrass earlier, George was thankful the man was nowhere to be seen George made his way into the inn and back to Grace. At his whistle, the bolt was drawn back, then the door opened a fraction and one pretty blue eye peered at him through the narrow aperture. She opened the door wider and let him in. "I thought it best to be cautious. You're back sooner than I expected. You must have swallowed your breakfast in double quick time."

"I haven't had any," George replied, as he bolted the door behind them. "Douglas is preparing a small picnic. We can stop and share it when we are away from here."

Grace's smile lit her face. "That is both thoughtful and kind of you. It may be unladylike to admit it, but I had little appetite for my supper in the parlour with Corbett for company last evening and am exceedingly hungry."

George moved to the unglazed window and inspected the slats of the shutters. "I guessed you might be."

On inspection, he found the slats were ill-fitting and the bottom two easily removed. He leant his weight on the frame and thought it strong enough to bear Grace's weight as she climbed down. The rope ladder was soon attached but he did not throw it over the windowsill, leaving it coiled on the floor. "I caught Corbett's wretched valet snooping around. I'll check he's not lurking. Let the ladder loose when you hear my whistle again and make your way to the barn."

"I wish you'd knocked Snodgrass out too." Grace frowned. "And the pair of them were locked safely away in the root cellar."

"Maybe," George countered, playing devil's advocate. "Or maybe the strength of two men would have been enough for them to break down the door, and we'd have the pair of them on our heels."

"True," she agreed and let him out of the public privy once more.

George walked to his bedroom then packed his portmanteau. It did not take long. He travelled with luggage small and light enough to be attached to the back of Sampson's saddle by way of a leather strap. He pulled Grace's bonnet from under the bed and put in in his luggage, but left the now useless parasol. It would no doubt be found sometime in the future, when whoever discovered it would wonder how such a thing could have got there.

The landlord was bustling between the taproom and kitchen when George made his way downstairs and paid for his stay. As he picked up the wrapped parcel Douglas offered him in exchange, he noticed Snodgrass sitting in the taproom drinking from a small tankard of ale. George nodded over his shoulder at the valet. "Keep him out of my way for the next half hour, will you?"

Douglas inclined his head. "I'll do so gladly, my lord. He's not the type to say no to the offer of an ale on the house, I suspect."

George thanked him, returned outside and whistled his two notes under Grace's open window. He chuckled when it was returned from above. Her hidden facets were manifold. The rope ladder snaked down. Grace grinned at him as she emerged, her skirt and petticoats kilted at her knees, her lower legs, clad in cotton stockings, on full display.

"Shocking, Mrs Foston," he teased. "I thought you said hoyden, not hussy."

"Don't look if you're offended, Mr Armstrong," she shot back. "Avert your eyes."

George folded his arms and leant his weight against a tree trunk. "No offence taken here, none at all. I'm assiduous in making sure you do not slip. Anyway, I'm enjoying the view."

"Rake!"

"Hellcat!"

He straightened when her feet touched the ground and offered her his hand. "We are very well matched, then."

Grace put her hand in his without replying but a light blush coloured her cheeks which delighted him probably more than it should. *She feels the attraction as much as I do.*

"So..." — he smiled — "as far as anyone is concerned I'm off to the sheep sales."

"But what happens when you're not seen there?" she asked in a worried voice. Her teeth scraped her bottom lip, and George was hard- pressed not to replace them with his own and kiss her long and hard.

Neither the time nor the place.

"If your absence is noted," she added, "could it backfire on you?"

"No one can expect to see everyone they should in such a melee," George assured her. "At times I have almost walked by a well-known acquaintance and not noticed him. All will be well. When we reach my friends' home we will be able to relax for a short while. Then we will press on and rest at an inn."

He led her into the cool semi-darkness of the barn where the two horses waited — as he'd requested, saddled — and strapped his portmanteau to his mount after removing Grace's bonnet from it. Her hat's sojourn in his luggage had left it somewhat crumpled, and he apologised as he handed it over. "Sorry, but I couldn't be seen carrying it in my hand inside the inn."

She surveyed the damage and shrugged as she put it on. "It'll do. It was in no way a favourite of mine."

The smaller horse, a dappled mare, whinnied, and he introduced Grace to her ride. "She is called Posy. And the handsome fellow behind her is Sampson. Let's get you mounted, and we can head towards Duncan and Cairstine's, where I'd like to exchange these horses for two which haven't been seen in this the vicinity. It would have attracted notice had I requested a lady's saddle. Can you ride astride?" He hoped so, for it would enable them to travel at a quicker pace.

Grace smiled. "I can, as it happens. It is so much more comfortable even if it is looked upon askance by many, although I normally wear a modesty apron to spare the blushes of folk who would otherwise be shocked at the sight of my lower limbs."

George looked around for something like a horse blanket that could be made to fit the task. "There must be something we can use…"

Her smile widened as she side-eyed his lower half speculatively. "If you just happened to have another pair of trews…"

He laughed, pulled the garment from his portmanteau and handed it over. She made a circular motion with her index finger. He duly shuffled around and presented her with his back then listened to the enticing rustling of feminine apparel being raised. He nearly laughed out loud at the sight of her after she called, "I'm ready."

He turned back around to see she had mounted Posy without his assistance and was sat astride with a froth of petticoats and dress bunched around her thighs, while his inexpressibles, knitted to mould to his much-larger-than-hers frame, flapped around her legs. The excess material had done the trick, making her limbs barely discernible, but he found the overall effect highly comedic, especially as her bonnet was slightly askew. He bit down on his lip. "Very effective."

She chuckled. "Certainly. For people will be too busy picking themselves up off the floor for laughing so hard to have time be offended. Mount up, my lord."

For her beauty not to be accompanied by any measure of vanity was a refreshing change, and George smiled as he threw his leg over Sampson's back. "As ever, I am yours to command. My bill is settled. Let's put some distance between us and this place."

Grace nodded fervently. "I couldn't agree more. The further away from here we get, the happier I will be."

George led the way out of the barn. In the yard a large tabby cat sat sunning itself on an upturned bucket, and it stretched as they trotted past. Grace chirruped in its direction. She'd always had cats as a child and rued the fact they made her husband sneeze.

Evidently George noticed her fond expression. "You like cats?"

"Oh yes. Until I married we always had them around. Sadly, my husband sneezes if one comes near him. So" — she shrugged — "no cats, and try as I might,

I cannot become as enamoured with a dog. Man's best friend perhaps, but not necessarily a woman's. Never mind, such is life."

George turned Sampson's head north as they trotted out of the yard. Grace did the same with Posy's and remarked, "I hope your friends won't mind us using them as we are planning to do."

"Our friendship is well established so I don't believe they will find it an imposition, nor be fazed by our unexpected appearance. Duncan is a true friend, and as such will be happy to help." He kicked Sampson on and picked up the pace. "Now, if we go this way, we can get several miles away from here in reasonable privacy."

"Then lead on. The further, the better." Grace let her horse follow his, and they moved swiftly between the trees on a seemingly aimless course, one which didn't follow any specific track but still led them north-west in the direction they needed to go. She settled deep into the saddle and pondered over the unusual happenings of the last few days, culminating in meeting George.

He was a strange man. As far as she could tell, he'd jumped to her aid with no thought of what the outcome might bring, or with any thought of recompense. Then to agree to help her further—and indeed, set up the best way for that to happen—was something she thought few people would bother to do. Whatever the outcome, she would be forever in his debt.

As the trees thinned he slowed, turned Sampson and waited until she came alongside. "If my memory serves me correctly, we could ride uphill to a spot overlooking the river and rest our horses. Then eat our picnic relatively unseen, while being able to see a goodly way ourselves. The nearest coaching road is several miles to the south, then there's a drover's road over yonder ridge."

Grace nodded, content to let him and their horses set the pace. It was peaceful and quiet, and she took the chance to think about the last few days. Was there anything she could have done better? She didn't believe so, but George's intervention had given her food for thought. It was galling to admit, even to herself, that his coming to her aid had been both timely and helpful. When she'd blithely set out on her quest to save her sister, she really hadn't thought about all the ramifications. Or realised just how determined Corbett was. Thank goodness she hadn't confessed all of her plans to her husband. He would have been aghast and begged her to reconsider. As he was not in the best of health, she more than likely would have acquiesced.

Then where would her sister be?

So involved with her musings, it was several seconds before she realised they had stopped moving and George was staring at her with a grin.

"Wool gathering?" he enquired. "Or worrying?"

"Oh," she said with a laugh. "A bit of both if I am to be honest. Is this where we stop?"

"It is," he affirmed. "As I mentioned, we have a good view of the surrounding countryside from here but cannot be seen. I can think of no better place to eat our late breakfast."

He helped her to the ground. Grace glanced around with interest while he secured their mounts' reins to a tree branch then retrieved a corked stone flask and wrapped packet from his luggage. Her tummy rumbled.

"Oops, I am evidently ready to eat. Where are we? I am not familiar with this area."

They were tucked just below the edge of an escarpment, overlooking a tree-dotted, steep-sided valley, at the bottom of which a ribbon of a track could be seen through the trees.

"About three quarters of the way to Duncan and Cairstine's house," George replied. "The road you can see leads towards Carlisle. It's not the most direct route to Gretna, but it's a possible one, so probably best avoided in favour of the lesser-used drover's track."

"Do you think we may have been followed?" The thought had been niggling her.

"I doubt it, not yet, but given we're dealing with someone as oily as Corbett, I think it wise to be cautious."

"That makes sense." Somewhat more reassured, Grace sat with her back to the rock, crossed her ankles in a most unladylike manner and gazed at the view in front of her. On the road below a coach and four moved like a scurrying ant, and to their left three sheep ambled along a faint track, then disappeared from view. It was what a poet would no doubt call bucolic, and what she thought of as typical northern England countryside. "I know you said we need to stop overnight, but when should we get to Gretna?"

"If all goes well tomorrow, early to late afternoon. If it was myself and Sampson, I could do it faster, but with the best will in the world Posy is only a hired work horse"

"It all seems a lot of trouble to foil one man, awful as he is. Although I hope my sister will be grateful." It caused Grace some discomfort that she now owed people her gratitude, and in George's case money — for her coin purse was securely locked in her portmanteau along with the rest of her possessions. So far he had put his hand in his pocket for the hire of her horse along with their breakfast, and there was still the bill for their overnight accommodation to be met. However, she had no choice but to rely on him to continue supplying the funds. She hastened to reassure him, "I'll repay you for my expenses when I'm reunited with my luggage, and if there's ever anything I can do for your friends they have only to ask."

"There is nothing to repay to either myself or them." George stretched out beside her and took a wedge of cheese. "Anyone I know would be happy to do anything to scupper Corbett's plans, whatever they happen to be. He is a thoroughly bad lot who is well on his way to the river tick. If we could be well rid of him, more people would be satisfied."

Grace nodded and picked up her own portion of cheese and bread. It was so pleasant, sitting in the sunshine as if they didn't have a care in the world.

As if there were no Corbett forcing her sister to marry in such a haram-scarum fashion…

As if she and George were a couple enjoying a carefree picnic…

She broke off that chain of thought in a hurry. They were not! Time to think of other things. One which was pressing. She sighed and collected their rubbish. "I'll just go and…" She waved her hands towards a clump of head-high bushes. "I won't be long."

He chuckled. "I will go the opposite way."

Within a few minutes Grace had made herself comfortable once more and returned to where they had sat to eat only to find George had stowed all signs of their alfresco meal away and was stood beside his mount. She thought his stance looked stiff, even somewhat wary, and his words confirmed it. "I can't be sure, but I think I heard the sound of bracken crunching underfoot."

She glanced quickly around and saw no one.

George's gaze followed her own. "It's probably nothing, but let's get on and keep our eyes open. We aren't far from Duncan's house now. I did wonder again if we should stop there, but it would put us several hours behind where I would prefer us to be first thing in the morning."

"Then we press on with your original plan," Grace said firmly, squashing her fears as best she could. Why on earth had she thought the deception would be easy—and not take too long?

Because I am a simpleton.

George must have caught her fear because he tipped her chin up with his fingers. "It will all work out, I'm sure. What are a few hiccups on the way? Treat it like an adventure."

Standing so close to him, a delicious scent filled her nose, and she took a deeper breath to drink more of it in. A soft smile lit his eyes, although she had taken care not to audibly sniff.

"Bergamot. I have the oil of it infused into my shaving soap. You like?"

Oh, so very much. Delicious. Edible.

A fanciful notion that she squashed immediately, instead focusing her attention on her own rumpled state. "I only wish I could say I smelt as sweet."

He leant nearer, and she swallowed hard as she felt his warm breath tickle the delicate skin beneath her ear. "You smell of honey and sunshine."

The urge to tilt her head and invite his soft lips to kiss her neck was nearly overwhelming. It had been so long since...

She pulled herself up short. There were other, more pressing things to consider at that moment. Such as their horses moving restlessly as if something were disquieting them.

Voices in the distance drifted towards them on the still summer air. George moved quickly, clasping his hands and boosting her into her saddle before springing up and throwing his leg over his own. She kicked Posy into motion and at a fast trot they began to put some distance between them and whoever was behind them.

Chapter Four

George kept a wary eye on their surroundings as they moved steadily north and west. His sense of danger was on high alert. Corbett aside, peril could lurk in the most innocuous places. Footpads, for instance, were not uncommon in the remoter areas of the countryside. Only the previous week a traveller had been waylaid a few miles south of Corbridge and relieved of his belongings, including a valuable fob watch. He had no intention of relaying the story to Grace, though. He would just be extra vigilant.

He slowed Sampson to walk as they approached an old quarry, where, he had been told — whether rightly or wrongly he had no idea — the Romans had hewn out stone for Hadrian's Wall. Their horses, especially Posy, needed a ten-minute breather at a slower pace before the last short but difficult stretch to Duncan and Cairstine's home. Grace caught up to him, pressed her hand into the small of her back then stretched. "A welcome break. I confess it has been a while since I rode for so long. I am unfit."

He risked a short, sharp glance at her trim figure and wished he could linger. "We better agree to differ."

She blushed, then laughed. "I thank you, but this last year my exercise has been severely curtailed."

George wouldn't have been a healthy, lusty male if he hadn't pictured the type of exercise he would like to indulge in with Grace, especially when she chuckled and added, "Indelicate of me as it is to admit it, I have to say my bottom is quite numb."

Mmmm… How indelicate it would it be if I offered to massage it?

"I confess I'm much in the same state," he confided, not wholly truthfully as his cock made a nuisance of itself inside his breeches. "But we have not far to travel now. Duncan and I hunted over this ground a couple of months back. Take care though, as the track now steepens considerably. Call out if you feel Posy is struggling."

She nodded, and to his relief Posy remained sure-footed over the rougher terrain as it climbed. He halted at the summit and pointed towards a long low barn tucked into the side of a slope of a hill. "Over there."

Grace looked adorably confused. "Your friends live in a barn?"

"No." He chuckled, then explained, "Their house is screened by the trees behind it. The barn is where we leave the horses. It might sound what Mr Keane would call on stage somewhat cloak and dagger-ish, but if you wouldn't feel slighted by my asking you to wait in the barn with them, I will walk to the house and fetch Duncan and Cairstine. If I relay the bare bones of our story to them while I bring them to meet you, their exclamations of surprise…and there are bound to be some...will be made away from the ears of any gossiping servants."

"Well, I'm all for being inconspicuous," Grace said fervently. "Introductions can wait. I'll take the opportunity to remove your breeches—" She broke off. "That came out wrongly. The breeches I am wearing which belong to you not... Oh, stop it."

George was laughing. "I am sorry, but I agree it came out wrongly." *More is the pity.*

"I will tidy myself while you're gone," Grace finished.

They trotted on and entered the barn. The interior of the building was dim. A few motes of dust danced in the air, highlighted by the faint sunshine which entered through the open door. Grace jumped from her saddle unaided and crooned as she stroked her filly's nose, "Who's a good girl, then? Shall we find you a sugar lump or carrot?"

George dismounted with a grin, took both sets of reins and led the horses to a stall. "You might find what you're looking for in the feed bucket by the door. Bring a reward for Sampson too? I'll get them unsaddled then head up to the house. I will whistle like this when we come back." He gave a long low two-toned whistle. "If you are happy, will you do the same?"

Grace stuck her nose in the air and flapped her hands at him. "I will, now off you go. You are not the only one capable of unsaddling your own horse. And don't show your face here again for at least half-an-hour."

He laughed, took the hint she required a little privacy for a while and left her. A five-minute walk saw him happily ensconced in the comfort of an overstuffed leather armchair in Duncan's study with a pewter tankard of ale in his hand to slake his thirst. Cairstine, perched on the arm of her husband's matching armchair, smiled as George drank deeply.

George wiped the froth from his upper lip. "I have a friend with me. I've left her in the barn."

Cairstine's smile widened as she quizzed him. "A lady friend? In the barn? That you can't present at the house? Very mysterious. Do tell!"

He opened his mouth to do so, then noticed Duncan's frown. "Ah… Your friend wouldn't happen to be rather noticeably beautiful? Golden-haired? The type of lady that once glimpsed is not easily forgotten?"

An apprehensive shiver passed down George's spine. "She might just fit your description. How did you come by it?"

Duncan sat straighter. "One of the servants returned from an errand in town this morning with news of a hue and cry having been sent up for a couple who absconded from a coaching inn without settling their bill. Some unfortunate soul realised what they were up to and attempted to detain them. They locked him in a cellar in order to escape apparently, and now he's furious and out for blood. A reward has been offered for information as to the couple's whereabouts."

Damn Corbett! He's escaped ahead of time.

"And the male protagonist?"

Duncan eyed him up and down, his lips quirking with the start of a grin. "Brown hair, tall, muscular. Highly dangerous. Not to be approached. Information is all that is required to secure the reward."

Double damnation! The snake! I might have guessed he'd do something so tricky.

George steepled his hands together. "Well, the gossip is correct on that point. Any person attempting to remove Grace from my care will meet with all the force necessary to prevent them. The absconding without paying my shot is incorrect, as the landlord could tell anyone. If the details of the inn were provided, which I suspect they were not. I wonder, whereabouts is the information to be deposited?"

Duncan smiled. "To be confided to a Mr Snodgrass, who can be enquired for in the posting inn on the road to Carlisle."

How the devil did Corbett guess the lady he knows as Jane would still head north instead of hightailing it home?

That thought would have to remain a question for future speculation, as Cairstine regarded him with raised eyebrows and a mischievous glint in her eye to enquire, "Grace?"

It was time to come clean, and he gave them a succinct precis of the story so far. Duncan's brow knitted in concentration. "Well, I can't say I'm surprised to learn Adrian Corbett is the villain of the piece. The Corbetts are an unreliable bunch, with a well-deserved reputation for changing sides at the drop of a hat."

George guessed which way Duncan's thoughts were heading. "Bonnie Prince Charlie's attempt to regain his throne in forty-five?"

Duncan nodded. "Corbett's birth line descends from one Robert Corbett, Provost of Dumfries. A Scot who locked the city gates of Dumfries against a Scottish Stuart claimant to the throne in favour of changing sides and supporting the English instead. He can anglicise the spelling of his name all he likes, but his birthright is as Scottish as mine. A family of turncoats, are the Corbetts."

George drained the last of his ale. "The man has a bad reputation around town for underhand dealings and welching on his bets. He's a despicable rogue who will not be getting his grubby little mitts on Grace."

Cairstine smiled. "May we meet her now?"

He set his tankard down and stood. "Of course. She required a little time to restore her travel-worn appearance, and I'm sure she must have done so by now."

They followed him from the room and over to the barn. He whistled softly, the two-tone note Grace would recognise, and was relieved to hear her reciprocating response. All must be well. He called as they reached the door. "Grace? I have Duncan and Cairstine with me."

Grace set down the stone flask, now empty of cold tea, and stood as the new arrivals entered the barn. The lady, slim with red-red hair braided into a bun on the nape of her neck, walked to Grace and gave her a hearty hug.

"Don't be alarmed," she said with an underlying hint of a soft Scottish burr. "George has confided your story, and we've had a servant return from town with news of a hue and cry being set up for a couple who left an inn without paying their shot. There is no one in this house who would give your presence away if told not to, but for the best, you should probably consider altering your appearance before you take to the road again."

"Oh, goodness." Grace turned to George. "What a guddle I have set up. I am so sorry, but I had no other ideas on how to approach the dilemma Jane was in.

Now I seem to be involving more and more innocent people."

Cairstine snorted. "It's a long while since Duncan has been called innocent."

He grinned. "Or you, my friend."

Cairstine curtseyed and laughed. "Thank you. Also true."

"We'll get you to Gretna and your sister. Cairstine will provide all the assistance you require." Duncan smiled. "It will be our pleasure, especially to help thwart Corbett."

George smirked. "There's always the britches…"

"The very thing!" Cairstine exclaimed, clapping her hands together. "Why did I not think of it? You should adopt the appearance of a young man, Grace. I don't know about George's breeches, but Duncan's mother never discarded a thing, and there's a trunkful of clothes in the attic from his youth."

"And me?" George asked. "I don't think I could pass as a female."

Grace eyed him up and down. The epitome of hot-blooded and handsome masculinity.

Nor do I.

"Probably not." Cairstine sniggered as Duncan rolled his eyes. "Well, being as you're looking a little travel-stained rather than your normally pristine self, we'll rough you up a little more, and you can be the slightly-down-at-the-heel teacher escorting your charge north to continue his education under the auspices of St Andrew's University."

"Young Master Timothy and his tutor, Mr. Brownlow, it is then," Grace agreed briskly, then nearly laughed at the consternation written large all over George's face. For someone known for his fastidiousness and perfect tailoring, she suspected the next day or so would be agony. She held out her hand. "Come along, Mr Brownlow. I believe my tresses are somewhat too long for my role, so I need a haircut, and your own hair needs mussing up."

He didn't look any happier at her pronouncement but complied with a wry smile. Grace's own smile slipped a little when they followed along behind their hosts and she caught sight of their home. There was only one word for it and that was grand—and not just rich grand, but passed-down-the-generations grand. She nudged George with her elbow and whispered, "Just who did you say your friends are? I seem to have missed their surname."

He smiled. "You seemed nervous of your welcome, so I omitted it until you'd met them. This is but one of the houses owned by the Earl and Countess of Callander. It's not their main country seat, of course, but Duncan and Cairstine prefer to spend their time in the cosiest of their three residences. This one, and their hunting lodge in the Trossachs."

Grace took another look at the expansive crenulated edifice. "Cosy? At thirty or more rooms? I'm not much accustomed to moving in such rarefied circles, you know."

"Neither was I, but Duncan and Cairstine are as down to earth as anyone I know. You will find no high-handedness due to rank when in their company."

Somewhat reassured, Grace put her best foot forward, and they were soon ensconced in a sunny parlour inside the house. Cairstine retrieved a pair of pinking shears from the workbox beside her chair and George winced with every snip of the shears Cairstine wielded on Grace's locks.

Grace, though, felt lighter as her curls fell to the floor, and giggled when she saw the unruly mess of various lengths in the mirror when Cairstine laid the scissors down. How strange such a simple act could change an appearance to such a degree. She ran her fingers through the feather-like weight of her tresses. "What do you think?"

Cairstine patted her on the back. "You look totally different. I swear it gave me shudders to do something so terrible on purpose, but it will be worth it, I'm sure."

"I hope so." George ran his hands over his uneven hair, which Cairstine had roughed up. "Even my gamekeeper is tidier than this, and he is not at all particular in his habits."

"In the meantime," Duncan said prosaically, "while you ladies rummage through my boyhood clothes, we men will adjourn to the dining room, and you can join us at your leisure."

That being agreed, Grace followed her hostess up the stairs.

"Can you adopt a local accent to cement your disguise?" Cairstine asked. "Dumfriesshire would be ideal if you can manage it?"

Grace grinned and looked her straight in the eye. "Aye, bonnie lass, I can."

Cairstine chuckled. "Wonderful. How on earth?"

"One of the maids when I was growing up. She was the orphaned wee sister of our cook and came to live with us. We were much of an age, and you know how easily children mimic the way others speak. I'm not saying it is specific to any area but I think it will do. I can also do a passable Irish accent from my papa's love of horseflesh and our Irish coachman."

Cairstine waggled her eyebrows, her voice guttural and low. "In time wiz ze music, if you please, *mein fraulein.*"

Grace laughed, and Cairstine clarified, "Papa engaged a German music master when I was ten. His brows jumped up and down in perfect time to the beat." She lifted the lid of a large dusty trunk and sneezed. "I need the maids to come in here. Before everything is hidden under a heap of cobwebs. Now let us delve and see what we can find."

The trunk yielded exactly what they were looking for — a pair of nankeen britches, a shirt, a woollen jacket and a peak-brimmed felt hat.

Cairstine held them up and examined them. "No moth holes. Thank goodness. Who knows when these were last worn *or* cleaned, but they will do."

"More than." Grace changed and rolled her undergarments into her dress. Her rather feminine boots, she decided, would have to be worn, for there was no alternative footwear that fitted her.

Cairstine gave her approval. "I think you'll pass muster. Boots are boots, and the jacket is ill-fitting enough not to show the outline of your breasts. Shall we see what the men think?"

Grace nodded. She couldn't help but smirk when two sets of male eyes widened as she and Cairstine entered the dining room.

"Well, just look at you, my laddo." Duncan chuckled. "'andsome, young man."

"Good Lord..." George spluttered, while giving her the sort of look guaranteed to make her skin tingle. "Perhaps you best not eat too much. Those clothes are rather snug."

"Not a chance of abstinence," Grace retorted, both pleased by his look and annoyed at how instantly her body reacted to him. She diverted her attention to the table laden with a joint of ham, a whole roasted chicken and a fine Stilton cheese accompanied by a basket of bread, soft yellow butter and a damson tart. Her belly gave notice of her recent shortage of rations with a noisy rumble. "I must admit, I'm quite hungry."

Cairstine took her seat. "Come and eat so you two can be on your way and arrive before it is dark. The Rising Sun Inn is small but remote so it should not be full."

Replete after half an hour, Grace pushed her plate away. "Thank you. Both the food and the company have been wonderful."

Duncan smiled. "You're very welcome. George suggested a change of horses would be in order, so to fit with your new personas, I'll ask Jamie to make the pony and trap ready."

* * * *

Two hours later they drove sedately into the stable yard of the inn just as the sun was setting. A little later in the day than George had originally predicted but, he reasoned, all the better. *Less people about.* He looked around as an ostler appeared at the run. "Sorry, sir, didnae think anyone else was due."

"Later than I hoped. You seem somewhat busier than we anticipated."

The ostler indicated an open door. "Ah, the sheep sales is on, but the landlord's through there if ye wanna try yer luck."

George nodded and led Grace into the cool hall then rang the bell on the long sideboard. "Let's hope the innkeeper is still able to accommodate us."

The landlord approached, looked them up and down and answered with barely concealed impatience at being interrupted by persons of such little consequence. "We's overrun with travellers inspectin' the livestock at thon sale. Ah've a single room wa a truckle bed and if ye take it ye can count yersels lucky. Payment up front."

Grace nearly giggled when George's face pokered up, but he managed to stay in character as he handed over a shilling and answered, "I thank you, kind sir. My charge and I are on way north to the university where he will complete his education. Your offer is accepted and much appreciated."

The landlord grunted and clicked his fingers at a hovering lad. "Number three. Show 'em up."

The room was clean and plainly decorated, although small. The bed was not ungenerous, but the truckle-framed straw mattress at the foot of it looked designed to accommodate a small child, and apart from a small washstand, there was not another item of furniture to be seen. Grace surveyed their sleeping arrangements after the lad had left the room. "I think I can fit on the truckle if I curl my legs up tight."

George walked over and looked for himself. "You will have cramp in the morning if you do so. The bed, although not overlarge, is big enough to be shared. If I place the bolster pillow down the middle to divide us, we could manage, don't you think?"

Grace swallowed hard. *So close.* However, George was right. After the unaccustomed exercise of riding astride, her muscles would spasm if she spent the night scrunched up tight, and her legs would be painful to walk on come the dawn. She nodded and there was a knock on the door.

George opened it. The lad was back, and he held a plate of victuals and a jug of ale. "Master says as do yer want a wee bittie mutton pie an' a jug o' ale? It'll cost ye a tanner if ye do."

George put his hand in his pocket and dug out the required coin, then added a couple of coppers for the lad who had brought it. Grace pulled off her cap and tossed into the corner of the room when the door shut behind him, then ran her fingers through her hair.

"Argh, that is better. I hate wearing headgear." She sat on the bed and bounced up and down a little to test the mattress. If not for the seriousness of her sister's predicament, she would have called it the most enjoyable day she'd had in a long, long time. Duncan and Cairstine had been so welcoming, and she couldn't help but admit how good it had been to converse and laugh with people nearer her in age than she normally encountered in her daily life.

George sat down on the other side of the bed, and although they had eaten a hearty meal earlier, the pie was soon demolished and the jug emptied.

The long day caught up with Grace and she yawned behind her hand. George set the plate and jug on the floor. "There's only the public facilities, I'm afraid. I'll go in search of them first and ensure they're in good order."

Grace contemplated her sleepwear while he was gone. She wore no undergarments—they, along with her dress, were currently stowed in his luggage, which they'd left in the trap. Still, to remove her jacket and spend the night in her britches and shirt was more decent than donning a silky, thin chemise, she decided.

George returned a few minutes later. "Down the hallway, third door on the right. The inn may be full, but thankfully, the dunny has been recently emptied."

It was not only clean and mercifully nigh on empty, but it also smelt reasonably fresh. Possibly due to the foresight of someone who had placed a huge bunch of hedgerow herbs in one corner of the room. Even so, Grace had no inclination to linger and was soon on her way back to their room — luckily without encountering any other guest, although voices could be heard behind some of the doors.

Pray they stay where they are.

When she entered their bedchamber, George had pulled back the coverlet and pushed the feathered bolster lengthways down the middle of the bed. "I'll turn away while you get comfortable," he told her. "Let me know when I am allowed to turn around again."

"Of course." Grace removed her jacket, got into bed and pulled the coverlet up to her chin. "I'm ready. You can come." Then she cursed under her breath. Her words hadn't sounded as innocent as she'd intended so she added, "My eyes are shut. You can get in." She rolled on to her side and faced the wall, unsure if what she had just said made her previous statement sound better or worse. George's footsteps echoed as he walked across the room, then the empty side of the bed dipped as he lay on the mattress beside her.

Was he naked? Did he wear a nightshirt? Did he snore very loudly? Did she? Grace's mind was awhirl with questions, not any of which she could find the answer to.

Do not think of it. Go to sleep…

She willed herself to breathe evenly and within seconds George's breathing was as regular as hers. His solid presence beside her was reassuring. She relaxed, enjoying the nearness of him, even with bolster between them, and her eyelids fluttered closed…

* * * *

The heat of a full sun warmed her skin through her clothes as she skipped amongst the long grasses of the meadow. A bee hummed nearby, gathering nectar from the wild flowers dotted throughout the tall, green fronds. A spark of happiness ignited deep within her.

Peace… Quiet… Warmth… Escape…

All luxuries in short supply inside a house that had once been a happy home, before Mama had passed and Papa had remarried. She dropped to her knees then lay on her back hidden from view, and once again searched her memory for anything she and Jane might have done to cause their stepmother to dislike them so. As usual, she came up with nothing other than they intruded on Papa's time when he was home, which unfortunately was not often.

Matters improved when he was but in his absence, under the auspices of careful household management, their diet consisted of scrag end of mutton, boiled pudding and thin watery soup. Worse was the instruction to sit for hour after hour stitching 'improving' samplers in a house where no fires were permitted, even in the depths of winter. These edicts did not apply to her stepmother's personal rooms, where a roaring blaze burned night and day. She was the only person who could spend where and on what she chose. That didn't extend to anything but the bare necessities for her stepchildren. When her stepmama had declared the upkeep of non-working ponies was an expense which could not be borne, the sisters' childhood mounts had been sold at the autumn horse fair.

She had to stop thinking about the woman. Tears welled and, irritated, she dismissed her stepmother from her mind. She would not spoil a rare hour or two of freedom on this beautifully warm, sunny day. Instead, she shut her eyes to indulge in her favourite daydream.

He would be handsome, of course. The suitor who one day soon would ride up to their house and demand her hand in marriage. Good natured, with a twinkle in his eye that was reserved for when he looked only at her.

The perfume of wild flowers drifted to her nose, and she tried to place it. Bergamot sprang to mind, although she had no idea where from. So far as she knew it wasn't a species she'd ever seen growing in the local vicinity.

Her future lover did not yet have a name, but his lips were soft on hers when he kissed her. She could feel his breath, sweet and warm, as their tongues entwined. His mouth moved down her neck, then to her breast, and fastened on the hard nub of her nipple. Her breath hitched at the sensation, the secret intimate place on her body longing for his touch, and she parted her legs. His fingers explored and caressed the wet creases he found there.

"George…yes…"

Her lover now had a name, and he knew hers too.

"Grace… Sweetheart…"

The intensity of her yearning increased as his elegant fingers stroked and played. She reached for the hard rod pressing against her thigh and his breathing quickened.

"Are you sure, my love?"

Desire throbbed through her pelvis. Urgent. Demanding.

"Please…yes…"

He lay over her, and she wrapped her legs around his thighs. He groaned and eased the tip of his shaft inside her channel. She mewled with pleasure as he plunged deeper. It *felt so good, their coupling undeniable and natural, as if preordained. Faster, harder. She writhed beneath him, the ecstasy of rapture approaching then exploding through her belly. He thrust, again, again and again until with a low deep-throated growl he tensed and stilled...*

Warm and comfortable, Grace wasn't sure what woke her until she felt the tickle of hair on her cheek. She opened one eye to see the grey light of dawn. Why was her head resting on George's bare chest?

Consciousness returned. Oh, Lord! She'd been dreaming, and it had been one of *those* dreams. The type where you woke with your hand between your legs... But this time? She risked a peep down the length of the bed. The bolster pillow lay at the foot of it, along with her nankeen trews. Her shirt was still in place, although unbuttoned, and the muscular, hairy limb resting against her own confirmed George was naked below the waist too. The scent of him filled her nose — an enticing hint of male muskiness overlaid with bergamot. She knew then, in the state betwixt sleep and wakefulness, her burgeoning love for him had been set free. It had been *she* who had kissed him first, had said his name — and he'd responded. Their lovemaking had been mutually passionate. He'd called her 'my love' and 'sweetheart' — and that was true on her behalf too.

How I wish... But it cannot be...

George stirred and opened his eyes. "Good morning, my lovely lady. Perhaps a kiss to start the day?"

A tear trickled down Grace's cheek. "I dare not. For if I do, I will never be able to leave you, and I know I must."

The pain in her heart was mirrored in George's eyes as he reached out and wiped the tear away with the pad of his thumb. "I know, my love. One night of passion to last a lifetime is how it must be. Much as we would wish it different."

Grace nodded numbly. Her heart shattered into a thousand pieces as she reached for her britches.

George counted to ten and waited for the ache in his cock to subside. Once his hopeful shaft had got the message there would be no sweet early-morning lovemaking, he slid from the bed and replaced his clothes. Resolutely, he didn't sneak another glance in Grace's direction as she tidied her hair. Even cut as it was, he thought it was lovely and suited her.

Everything about her was in his eyes, yes, perfection.

If what we did was wrong, why was it so perfect? But it is and must be...over. Stop thinking about it. Which was easier said than done. He tugged on his boots.

As he tied his cravat, and Grace put on her cap, an uproar outside the inn made them both jump.

"What on earth?" George walked to the window of the bedchamber and set it ajar by a couple of inches, which made it easier for him to observe the entrance to the stable yard and some of the road beyond. The area was deserted, but as hoofbeats and shouting grew louder the ostler, along with the landlord, erupted from the inn, no doubt to discover what was amiss. A sweating horse galloped round the corner of the road and was yanked to an abrupt halt by its rider.

He leaned down and pointed at the landlord. "You there! I seek news of two travellers. One female, attractive, blonde, the other male, dark-haired of good build. A bit of a ruffian."

Corbett! Blast him! George moved back an inch. Not that he thought Corbett would look upwards, but better to be safe than sorry.

The landlord seemed disinclined to reply to this stranger's hectoring tone. He folded his arms and stared in stony silence.

"Answer me, damn it!" the rider shouted, his face choleric. "My ward has been abducted. Have you seen her, with or without him?"

Grace came up beside George and peeped over his shoulder with a frown. "Corbett? Already?"

"So, it seems. Shh, let's listen."

"Eh?" The landlord still appeared to have no immediate inclination to answer Corbett's question. "Your what?"

"Dolt. Answer me now or…or…" Corbett scowled and didn't deign to finish his sentence, but his stance seemed to persuade the innkeeper he'd best provide a more expansive reply than he had previously.

"There's nae females staying here, what w' the sheep sales being on an' all. Saw a couple like what you said a couple of days ago, though. Pretty blonde lady wi' a military man. Lotsa braid. Officer of some sort, higher than a captain from the gold on his uniform, I should say. They didn't stop the night. Just had a bite of dinner then got on their way. Were that 'er?"

Grace grinned at the look of confusion on Corbett's face as he grumbled. "Two days ago? Timing's wrong. Army man? Can't be them, then…"

The landlord gave Corbett a glare of hearty dislike. "I'm wonderin' how on earth did a wee bittie lassie go off with someone you describe as a ruffian, eh? Not very guardian-like, is it?"

"Nincompoop!" Corbett snapped. "I need ale to refresh my thirst before I ride on. Fetch me some."

The landlord turned his back with a couldn't-care-less shrug of indifference. "You want ale, come into the bar away an' fetch it yersel'. I'm nae your fetcher and carrier."

"You work here. You should serve me," Corbett complained loudly as he dismounted and tied his mount's reins to the standing post.

"I will when you gets to the bar."

Someone nearby sniggered. Corbett swung round but the only people nearby — a small boy and an ostler — stared at him innocently. He scowled.

"Argh, bumpkins, the lot of you. If I weren't so parched, I wouldn't bother…"

Grace mouthed 'Jane', then stepped back from the window with a smile. "I think we've won. If my sister and Major Winterbottom were here the day before yesterday, only a few hours from Gretna, they must be married by now."

George agreed, but with a note of caution. "I think so too, but we should make sure to get to Gretna ahead of Corbett so you can confirm the matter. Our bill is paid. Let's sneak out of here while he drinks his ale and arrange a small inconvenience to delay him."

A slow smile spread across Grace's face. "I like it. What did you have in mind?"

George beckoned her to return to the window and pointed to a clump of bushes growing on the side of the road twenty or so yards away from the inn. "We'll untie Corbett's horse and tether it there. Close enough for him to spot it and wonder if he secured it properly to the standing post. Hopefully he'll think the beast just wandered off in search of its own snack and come and retrieve it. I'll be concealed in the bushes to surprise him, then we'll see how far he gets once I've confiscated his boots and britches."

She grinned. "You're intending to leave him bare-arsed naked from the waist down?"

He smirked. "I certainly am. It's the least Corbett deserves for all the trouble he's caused."

Her chuckle lightened his sore heart a little. "He most certainly does. Let's do it."

The inn was throbbing with customers as they walked down the stairs and it was easy to pass through the crowd unnoticed. Corbett's mount seemed content to see anyone who wasn't Corbett and came with them willingly. A patch of lush fresh grass near the bushes added to the horse's happiness and with a soft whinny it lowered its head, allowing Grace to secure the animal on a long rein to a convenient branch.

George parted the bushy fronds and pushed his way through to the centre of the outcrop whilst Grace darted behind an oak tree to watch the proceedings, hidden behind its substantial trunk.

The minutes crawled past, but just as George suspected his calf muscles were beginning to cramp from his crouching down for so long, the horse whinnied — and it was not the soft sound of earlier, but a more high-pitched protest of approaching distress. George clenched his fists. He could imagine the type of owner Corbett would be and it was not a pleasant thought.

The swish of a riding crop came first, shortly followed by the slap of leather on horseflesh. "Wander off, would you, you ill-behaved bastard. Well, you shall learn your lesson not to do so again!"

Furious at the man for meting out such treatment to the unfortunate creature, George didn't hesitate. He launched himself upward before propelling himself forward to tackle Corbett around his waist. His momentum took them both to the ground, and George, as he'd planned, came out on top. He snatched the crop from Corbett's hand before the man could realise what was happening and use it on him. He was tempted to give Corbett a few hefty thwacks with it, but thought the better of it, and instead tossed the crop out of reach and snarled through gritted teeth, "There's only one bastard around here, and that's you."

"I'll...I'll..." Corbett struggled beneath him, his chest heaving, until George cuffed him around his ear.

"Lie still," George demanded. "You are no match for me."

Corbett groaned and stopped moving. George stood and beckoned Corbett to do the same. "Resist or make one move to run away, and I will lay you out cold as I did before. Do you understand?"

Corbett nodded and did so while whinging. "I don't know why *you* had to get involved. What did I ever do to you?"

George didn't bother to answer but pulled Corbett by his collar into the centre of the bushes and demanded, "Your boots. Remove them then toss them as far as they will go."

Corbett swallowed several times, opened his mouth as if to protest then clearly thought better of defying. Two boots went flying into the distance.

"Now your britches."

"W-w-what…?" For the first time Corbett sounded unsure, less cocky, as if he had suddenly realised the mess he was in.

"Take them off!"

Whether it was George's fierce expression or the menacing step George took towards him, Corbett complied until his pale skinny legs were exposed.

"Not a pretty sight." George snatched the britches from Corbett's hand and held them aloft.

"Throw them this way," Grace shouted. "I know what to do."

George threw the garment in the direction of her voice.

Corbett's gaze followed the flight of his britches, and his mouth dropped open when he viewed who caught them. "That's not a lad. It's Jane!"

"Maybe it is or maybe it's not," Grace teased as she shinned up an oak tree and tied Corbett's britches, flag-like, from an upper branch.

George laughed and, leaving Corbett with only the length of his shirt to cover his embarrassment, strode out of the greenery. "Well met, Mrs Foston."

She giggled and made her way downward as Corbett spluttered. "Mrs Foston? Who…? What…?"

Grace pulled off her cap and made the stunned man a theatrically courtly bow when she reached the ground. "The Honourable Mrs Grace Foston, at your service…or rather, at the service of my younger *sister*. Come, Lord Renfrew, let us hasten to the nuptial celebrations of the newly wedded Major and Mrs *Jane* Winterbottom."

George grinned and freed Corbett's mount with a slap on its withers. "Trot on. You'll soon find someone who will gladly take in a riderless horse without an owner."

The beast didn't need a second instruction and cantered away. George watched it go then offered Grace his arm. "Shall we depart?"

She skipped toward him and threaded her arm through his. "I think we should." They turned away in the direction of the inn.

Corbett's voice followed them. "You'll rue interfering in my business like this, Grace Foston. I'll make sure of it, you…you…bitc—"

George swung around. "You've got off lightly for what you've done, sir. If I find you inconveniencing Mrs Foston again, I will mete out to you the just deserts you so richly deserve." He took hold of Grace's arm. "Time we left. There is a very unpleasant aroma around here."

"What a slimy specimen of humanity." Grace shuddered as they walked back to the inn to collect their pony and trap.

"A toad of the first order," George agreed. "But like all others of his kind, now his underhand schemes have been exposed to the daylight, he will crawl back under his rock…" An idea occurred. "Although when we collect our pony and trap I might just mention we saw him exposed to the world and how shocking it was."

Grace sniggered. "Shocking in his lack of—" She put her hand over her mouth. "A slight lapse of decorum"

George roared. "Honest though. Right, let's get a move on. Gretna awaits."

Chapter Five

In some ways, Grace wanted the drive to Gretna to go on and on. In others she wished it were over. It was torture to be so close to George, and she pushed her bottom farther into the corner of her seat. Her wayward body and emotions had betrayed her once. She would not allow them to do so again.

Am I a hussy? A fallen woman? I don't feel like one. Although perhaps I should. If I could go back a day in time, would I change it?

She examined her heart, and the one and only night of passionate bliss that had ever come her way or was ever likely to, and knew the honest answer was no. She would not.

George glanced her way and frowned. "Something is troubling you?"

She would not admit it and just sighed.

He shifted the reins into one hand and lifted his other arm as if to pull her to him and console her. She shrank away, and he dropped his arm with a sad smile. "Do you wish so much last night had not happened?"

Tears threatened. There were no words she could summon that would not cause them to fall so she merely shook her head.

George gazed abstractedly into the far distance. "No more than could I. Our lovemaking was all I ever dreamed of and more."

How she wished to say, 'and mine'. She didn't.

George shook the reins to urge the horse to pick up its pace. "Over yonder is Gretna. We will be there soon. What is done is done and will remain a beautiful memory between us. But from now, we must move on."

Grace huddled miserably in her corner of the seat until she spied two people walking ahead. She sat straighter. "Jane. Ahead with Major Winterbottom, Alfred. The lady in the blue walking gown."

"I see them." George tooled the pony and trap to arrive alongside the couple just as they slowed to watch a young child playing with a kitten.

Jane laughed as, with a rare show of public affection their papa would have frowned upon, she hugged Alfred. Her doing so was a balm to Grace's troubled soul. She *had* done the right thing to help her sister gain a happy and loving marriage and future life. That was the most important thing.

I have made my bed, and now must lie on it, however uncomfortable it may be.

Jane and Alfred slowed as if to cross the road. Jane turned and glanced incuriously at the approaching trap and its occupants.

Grace waved. "Jane, 'tis me."

"Grace?" Jane stared at her sister then the man next to Grace and finally back to Grace once more. She frowned. "What on earth are you wearing? Why have you chopped off your hair?" She nudged her companion. "It is Grace. Dressed as a boy."

Major Winterbottom's eyes twinkled as he stared. "So I see."

"With a stranger," Jane hissed. "Alone."

Grace noticed George's lips quirk. It was no laughing matter, but she understood that Jane's attempt at subtlety was not very successful.

"Why like this though?" Jane asked Alfred.

Why not ask me?

"My love, give Grace a moment to reply," Alfred said with a laugh. "There is no point asking questions if you give no chance for anyone to respond."

Grace glanced at George. "What should I do?" she asked in a low voice. "There is no space in the trap to invite them up, and we need to talk to them post-haste."

"Ask where they are heading, and we will meet them there as soon as we can." George held the restless pony in check. "We can't discuss things here."

"There's a lot to tell you," Grace said out loud. "Once we stable the pony where should we meet?"

Alfred smiled a little smugly. "My wife and I are staying at a nearby inn. 'Tis only a few hundred yards down this road."

Grace looked at her Jane's left hand and smiled at the sight of a shiny new band of gold encircling her sister's third finger.

Jane tutted and slipped out of her cloak. "Here. Put this on so you at least appear partially respectable."

Her tone told Grace Jane was going to demand a very full explanation indeed, and Jane's next words only added to her sense of foreboding. "In return, I also have some information I need to pass onto you."

Grace's heart missed a beat as she wrapped herself in the cloak. What news could Jane have to impart?

"Tell me, please?"

"At the inn," Alfred said quietly. "We are best to talk there, where I have bespoken a private parlour for myself and Jane."

Grace nodded with reluctance. He was of course correct, but how she hated waiting for the axe to fall.

"And you can tell me what has happened since we were last together," Jane said. She didn't add 'and who this man is', but Grace could sense the words hovering between them.

How do I tell enough to satisfy her without sharing things I most definitely do not want to explain? Some things were, without doubt, going to be left unsaid.

"Until then." George set the pony and trap in motion once more.

"Will you be able to assuage any doubts your sister may have that our endeavours have been carried out with the best of intentions?" he queried once they were out of earshot.

"I can only hope so. She can be somewhat like a terrier with a rat, but I will remind her what I did was for her happiness and no other reason."

George turned the equipage into the stable yard and drew up outside the inn door. The ostler ran out and stopped suddenly as he saw what he was expected to take charge of.

"Need ter book 'ere," he said roughly. "It's for the gentry, not any old bumpkin or prov...inshul."

"We are neither," George stated firmly. "Which if you had any sense you would recognise. Kindly take charge of the pony and trap. Our carriage and cattle suffered an accident. One has to arrive the in most convenient manner one can, be it not what one is used to." He threw the reins at the startled ostler who, in the face of hearing George's cultured tones, all of a sudden decided to be on his best behaviour and inclined his head in a respectful manner. George got down and held his hand out to Grace.

"Come, my dear. Let us makes ourselves known to the landlord and refresh ourselves while we await the arrival of Major and Mrs Winterbottom."

Grace took his hand, stepped out of the trap and added her mite to reinforce George's credentials. "After the trials of our journey thus far, I believe I am ready for a light repast, *my lord*."

* * * *

It was agony to watch — and listen to — the woman George knew he would love until the end of his days play down the intimacy that had developed between them as if he were a disinterested bystander coming to the aid of a lady in distress out of the goodness of his heart. He understood why this had to be so, but as Grace relayed a very shortened and simplified version of their escapades to Jane and Albert, how he wished he could stand up and proclaim his love for her.

He didn't. Instead he sat quietly supping his ale and nodding when appealed to, although he did not hold back when Grace summed up Corbett's actions.

"I will not apologise for appearing before you like this. It will not take long for my hair to grow back. A dress with the addition of a bonnet or linen cap until it does, and not a soul outside this room will know what I've done. Corbett had to be stopped. He's far more of an obnoxious toad than we even realised, Jane. The lies, the downright nastiness to those, man or beast, he considers beneath him..."

The bile rose in George's throat at the thought of the bastard even so much as touching his beloved's hand. "The man is an unscrupulous rogue. He's got off lightly this time. Should he cross my path in the future, he will not do so again."

"So, you see," Grace interjected quickly, "we were able to thwart Corbett and meet you here. Now, I have been patient. Tell me, please, what your news is?"

George held his breath, a strange lump in his stomach telling him whatever was coming next was not going to be in anyway palatable.

Jane bit her lip. "Not long after we arrived at Gretna a messenger arrived. Roger, not knowing the detail of the plan we had made between ourselves and believing you were merely chaperoning me to Gretna, presumed you were with us. Someone, we have no idea who, has approached him with information you are up to no good with some man or another. Roger threw him out with a flea in his ear but sent you, via us, a message to ask you to come home as soon as possible to scotch the rumours, although he was insistent you must stay until you had witnessed our wedding. I think we better hasten south with all speed. It is not right that our chance of happiness mars yours."

George listened to Jane's speech with growing dismay. Did that mean Grace was truly happy with Roger? Part of him wanted them to be happy, of course, but on the other hand...

There he stopped his train of thought. He *did* want Grace to be happy, but oh, how he wished it were with him! Now it appeared there would not even be a private goodbye between himself and Grace.

I need to be noble.

How he hated that expression. Noble indeed. How many of the nobility conducted themselves in a dignified way? He cleared his throat. "How can I help?"

Jane turned to him. "You *have* helped. So very much. I apologise for embroiling you in our affairs, my lord. I can only say I was at my wit's end and your assistance to my sister was, and is, very much appreciated."

Major Winterbottom stood and held out his hand. "I second my wife's sentiment, my lord. If at any time in the future I can provide similar assistance to yourself, call on me. Barring my duty to king and country, I am yours to command. Be assured we will do all we can to ensure your name is not brought into any of this *and* do our best to discover who is meddling and trying to cause trouble."

"I appreciate it, thank you," George replied. "I suspect Corbett will be behind it somehow, but I also suspect we will never know. With luck, once Grace is home and on show, so to speak, no more will happen."

George accepted the handshake but, noticing Grace's lip tremble slightly, didn't trust himself to speak further. He gave her what he hoped was a reassuring smile. *If only it could be a hug, or a caress.*

"We can but hope." Alfred smiled at his wife. "My love, if you could assist your sister to gather any items she requires for the journey, we can be on our way. I will pay our shot while you do so."

Grace glanced at George but spoke to Jane. "My change of clothing is on the trap. I will re-dress in your room?"

George swallowed hard as the three of them left the room. The time had come. There was no prolonging the inevitable. This was goodbye. He left the parlour and waited outside in the fresh air. The ostler brought round a carriage of the newest well-slung model. Grace would be back home in no time.

Grace and Jane walked out of the inn door with Major Winterbottom one step behind them. Grace left them, moved to George's side and brushed her lips across his cheek with a softly whispered, "I will never forget you or our time together. Now I must go." She swallowed heavily, and George was sure he could see dampness on her eyelashes.

Before he could speak, she took a small step away from him. "Take care and be happy."

The urge to pull her back to his side and hold her was nearly overwhelming but the moment had come to be honourably correct. He squared his shoulders and held out his arm. "May I escort you to your carriage?" *Then I will watch you fade out of my life, but not out of my mind. Never that.*

She nodded and allowed George to help her get settled. Jane bussed his cheek. "Thank you. I will take care of her from here."

George gave a brief nod. What else could he do? Now was the time to be stoic and accept what had to be.

It was only after the equipage carrying her away had disappeared around a bend that George realised he didn't know where she lived. Which, under the circumstances, was probably not a bad thing. South certainly, although he was reasonably sure she did not reside near Corbridge. He would have met Grace at some event or the other before this had that been the case.

George shuffled his feet, feeling somewhat at a loss as what to do with himself next. Good friends or not, the prospect of a fishing trip with Duncan and Cairstine had lost its appeal. Home to lick his wounds in private was the order of the day, he decided. He was not fit to be in the company of any other but himself.

Regroup, get rid of regrets and move on.

The outlay of a few guineas secured him a half-decent mount, and several weary solitary days later he was greeted warmly by Cairstine's father, Nathanial, the Duke of Glennard, when he arrived at Denny House—a rental property the duke had secured in order to pursue his own interests in Corbridge. Duncan's father-in-law chuckled at George's travel-worn state when he dismounted and presented himself in the drawing room. "The salmon not biting, are they? Or has m'daughter stamping her feet again in a strop seen you off?"

Cairstine's impetuous but short-lived temper being a source of family funning, George took the question with the pinch of salt it deserved. It was local lore that flame-red hair equated to a flaming temper, and Cairstine definitely lived up to that adage. "Not at all, my lord. The Earl of Callander and his beautiful countess were in fine form when I last saw them a few days ago. But my conscience pricks me. A night or two in your company while I check on the rebuilding of Armstrong House is what I'm after, if you'll have me? Then I'm away to the Cheviots to view the new additions to my flock."

The duke clicked his fingers. A footman jumped to attention and bowed. "Your Grace?"

"A bottle of brandy and two snifters. Baron Renfrew is in need of refreshment."

* * * *

Grace peered out of the window until George was lost from sight. The carriage was comfortable and rattling along at a good pace, but still her stomach churned and her heart was heavy. She sighed.

"You are very quiet," Jane observed. "I thought you would be cock-a-hoop. We achieved our aims. Stepmama and Corbett can trouble us no more. We are outside of their jurisdiction and our lives are now our own. I feel I need to pinch myself. There were occasions when I thought this day would never come."

Grace looked at her sister sitting contentedly alongside her new husband. Jane's happiness was palpable. "I am so pleased for you."

"Then why do you look as if someone has just stolen your new bonnet and trampled on it?" Jane asked. "What is wrong?"

Grace sighed. Something she seemed to be doing a lot of lately, and it annoyed her.

Snap out of it.

"I just sometimes wonder if I rushed into marriage without thinking it through. Did I truly understand all that would be expected of me? All it entailed? I suspect not. Perhaps if I'd shown some of your fortitude and maybe waited a little longer…"

Jane squeezed her hand. "I can't regret that you didn't. For if you had, you would not have been able to gift Blossom to me, who would not then have lost a shoe when I was riding over to visit you and Roger, and a certain handsome military man would not have come to my rescue."

Alfred stroked his moustache and smiled. "I almost didn't. You looked at me with such contempt."

"I did not," Jane protested. "I just had no idea what you were doing in such an out-of-the-way village. This handsome army officer and…"

She blushed, and Grace smiled.

I could have had what they have if only I'd waited.

It was not a thought to be voiced, so instead she asked, "How long will it take us to get to Old Clee?"

Alfred withdrew his fob. "Late tomorrow, with luck. The horses are fleet so we should not have to stop at an inn for more than one night, depending on the weather."

Grace nodded and his prediction came true. The weather was kind, the carriage, elegant and of the latest design, and the inn proved charming. A bath and the services of a maid restored her dress to a less travel-worn condition, but neither improved her mood, and the following morning her spirits dimmed with each passing mile. The air became noticeably fresher with a sharp tang of salt when they reached Old Clee on the Lincolnshire coast, and her home, Foston Grange, came in sight when they entered the village of Itterby.

Alfred refused her offer of refreshment on behalf of himself and Jane, preferring to push onto their married quarters, so she waved farewell to her sister with the promise they would meet up as soon as Jane was settled. Their major-domo, Colewell, waited to greet her at the front door. "It's good to see you back, madam. The master will be pleased. He's been a bit down with all the inclement weather we've had, but is better today."

She handed him her portmanteau. "Thank you, I'll go to him as soon as I've restored my appearance. Is he in his room?"

Colewell inclined his head. "As the doctor recommended. He rests after lunch." *And more often,* his tone inferred.

Grace nodded, ran upstairs and exchanged her travel worn gown for one of dimity cotton then hid her rough-cropped, shortened hair beneath a cap of linen and lace before making her way to the large corner bedchamber Roger used, with its panoramic view of the sea. He smiled as she entered his room.

"How lovely to see you again, my dear. The view outside is not very inspiring today. Too wild, I suspect, and I've missed getting into the garden. You look well. Did everything go according to plan?"

Grace kissed his papery cheek. Had he faded whilst she was away? "When did anything go according to plan?" she asked him lightly. "But we managed, even though it meant a few changes of tactics. Nothing drastic," she added in haste as Roger's brow puckered. "Jane and Alfred are now wed, and out of our stepmother's clutches. Now, tell me do, what is this cock and bull story going about with regards to me? Do I need to worry?"

She hoped she had pitched her tone light and airy, and showed she thought it of little consequence. It appeared she'd succeeded, because Roger chuckled.

"Nothing to worry you. A bad lot trying to make some money out of nothing, I suspect. I sent him on his way with a flea in his ear and a boot up the rear, courtesy of Thompson. Threatening all sorts, he was,

Thompson said. But as I told Thompson, threats mean nothing and whoever he is, he will soon become the laughing stock of the county if he continues to spread such farridaddle."

Grace settled Roger more comfortably onto his pillows. "Then I'm glad I'm home. I'll ring for tea, shall I?"

He sighed contentedly. "If you would, my dear."

* * * *

It was for the best she was back, she decided a few days later. Jane was delighted with the officer's quarters she and Major Winterbottom had been awarded. Her letters were full of how she filled her days and entreaties to Grace to visit them. However, to her sadness, although Roger appeared happy and contented, he was weak, and she could not leave him to accept her sister's invitation.

She filled her time reading to him then tiptoeing out of his room to attend to her household tasks when he dozed off. Life continued as it always had. Until two months later...

* * * *

The doctor called at the house, as he did every Monday, but this time his expression was unusually grave when he entered the parlour to discuss Roger's health.

"I'm sorry, Mrs Foston. I know there have been several false alarms and we've been down this road many times before, but your husband's pulse is weak. I wouldn't be doing my duty if I didn't warn you to prepare yourself for the worst. He would be better away from the coast, but I fear it wouldn't prolong his life for more than a few months."

Grace took a deep breath. "We have a house near Harrogate, and could go there now if you think..." She let her voice trail off.

"Ask him," the doctor advised. "I think it would be too much for him, but if his spirits are down... If he likes the idea, do it."

"Is there anything else I can do to help restore his strength? Beef tea? Hot flannels to his feet? Whatever is necessary. Just say."

Doctor Taylor walked closer, sat beside her on the sofa and patted her hand.

"Forgive me for taking the liberty of sitting without being invited to do so, but my duty is also to the living. Mrs Foston, your husband would not be with us now if it were not for your care of him over the last few years. He is much, much older than you. You have done all you can. Tell him your idea about Harrogate. Give him something to think about and perhaps look forward to. But I beg you, let him go to his rest when, as and where he wants."

Grace inclined her head. "I want him to enjoy what time he has left. I'll do as you say."

The doctor patted her hand once more, stood and left the room. She waited until the front door closed behind him then ran up the stairs to Roger.

He smiled when she suggested Harrogate.

"My dear, I would love it with all my heart, but...I fear the journey would be too much for you to cope with."

"Not me," Grace assured him as she watched his weak eyes brighten. "Shall I send word to the staff to ready it for us? We can leave whenever you think fit."

Roger struggled up on his pillows and a smile lit up the whole of his lined face. "Tomorrow?"

* * * *

"The move gave him these last few weeks of happiness," Grace said to Jane on the day of his funeral. "He enjoyed the many birds in the garden and admitted he'd often contemplated asking me to move here but believed I preferred the view of the sea. And I thought he did. Here it might be a grey, but it is not uniform, if you understand me." She waved her hand to indicate the weather.

It was as dismal as such an occasion deserved.

"He would have chuckled at the appropriateness of grey skies and black clothing, with the only colour coming from the grass and the robin over there on the blackberry bush." She sighed. "Life will be very different now."

Polite society deemed the service of final interment far too damaging to delicate female sensitivities for ladies to witness, so while Roger's took place, Grace sat in the parlour with Jane until the bell tolled its final conclusion, then handed out warmed wine to male attendees before retiring to bed.

A year of formal mourning was normally required. Roger had asked her not to follow tradition as, he had declared, black for such a length of time would be depressing. Grace had demurred, but finally agreed she would go into mauves and greys after three months and, if anyone queried her actions, tell them she was following her husband's written wishes.

Grace had ordered her widow's weeds accordingly and set about passing the time in arranging the house to suit her needs. It was only when her new dresses became increasingly tight that realisation dawned. Since her return home, her monthly courses had been absent. Then, in her belly, the babe kicked…

Chapter Six

One year later

George stared at his factor, McEwen, for several minutes. "What you're saying is that the man will not sell unless I go to speak to him in person?"

The factor grimaced. "So, it seems, my lord. Sir William has a reputation for both eccentricity and irascibility. He is determined that as he knew your father and was not overly enamoured by the man, he will not sell any of his prize flock to you without first meeting you and questioning you about your intentions."

McEwen fiddled with his quill, which he still held after rising from behind the office desk when George had walked in a few minutes earlier, waving a letter in the air and demanding what the factor knew about it. "Do you wish me to reply, my lord?"

George sat in the wing chair in front of the desk. "Damn the man. Surely he must know by now I am not like my father? I take good care of my staff, my estate and my animals. I neither imbibe snuff, drink to excess nor set the gossip columns of the press alight with any other form of antics."

In fact, since I returned from Scotland, my cock has seen so little action it is a wonder it has not shrivelled and died.

A climax by his own hand no longer interested him. He would occasionally find nature had taken its course after he woke if Grace had entered his unconscious dreaming, but no other female stirred his loins in the slightest. It was just one of those things. No Grace, no interest. He gave a rueful chuckle. "Perhaps I am too stuffy for him?"

McEwen smiled. "I very much doubt that, my lord. From the little I know of Sir William, I would guess he is a lonely old man who needs to raise some cash but is loath to let go of any of his flock. However, if needs must, he would welcome a little company whilst in the process of selling some stock."

George steepled his arms and tapped his fingertips together. "Then I suppose I must go to Leyburn and oblige him. What engagements do I have for the next week or two that I can't put off?"

McEwen, who was in practice also George's secretary, flipped open a large diary on his desk. "You are doing the bible reading at church on Sunday, and I presume you have not forgotten you're engaged to attend Lady Carruthers' supper dance this evening."

George grimaced. "Why on earth did I accept the invitation?"

"Her son begged you."

"Ah." George remembered the conversation with Harry Carruthers, who had said he needed an ally to help him ward off ambitious young ladies and their mamas. As the local belief was George was a dyed-in-the-wool bachelor, most young ladies saw him as someone to hone their flirting skills on, no more. "Damn Harry. Why he doesn't just give in and ask one of them to marry him I have no idea."

McEwen raised one eyebrow, and George laughed. "Yes, I accept that is a bit rich coming from me. Anything else?"

"There is nothing else of note in the diary until the village fundraising for the new almshouses ten days hence, on the twenty-third."

"Very well. Then I'll head south after I've fulfilled my duty at church. If you would send a missive to Sir William to inform him of the fact? I doubt my business with the man will take long. I'll ensure I'm back a day or two before the fundraiser."

"Of course, my lord."

George nodded his thanks and headed to the stables. He needed fresh air, especially if he had to suffer an evening he was sure he would find tedious. He knew Lady Carruthers' supper dances of old. The food might be good, but the dances were predictable, ditto the guests, and there would be no card tables to alleviate his boredom. If it weren't for his long-standing friendship with Harry he'd cry off.

As that wasn't possible, he'd ride his fidgets out first and suffer the supper dance with as much good humour as he could muster.

* * * *

In the end the evening was no way as dismal as he had anticipated. Susannah, married to Harry's cousin,

Viscount Statham, collared him soon after he arrived with a heartfelt '*phew*'.

"George, thank goodness. Will you save me?"

"From?" George bussed cheeks with Susannah, whom he had known from birth and thought of a sister. "You are, of course, mine to command."

She snorted. "Ha, that is as likely as there being a man in the moon, but your presence will divert any predatory male who believes that, as my beloved is serving on the continent, I am bored and easy game. I am neither. If I hadn't been expecting our first child when he received his orders for the regiment to depart, I would have travelled to the continent to be near him. Now I just wish him home. Both John and I miss him. Poor John, he is nigh on a year old and has never seen his papa. However, be that as it may, I am not in the market for a lover. Why do men assume widows, those with absent spouses, or those whose husbands are infirm would welcome…" — she blushed — "you know. So, will you help?"

Why did her words cause his thoughts stray to the forbidden compartment in his heart? The place where he kept Grace.

Did I cause Grace a similar problem? Surely not. Love, not lust, brought us together.

He offered Susannah his arm. "Come, between us we shall see the rascals off. Hold on tight and don't forget to titter at me now and then."

"Titter? Good lord. I'm not sure I know how." She laughed and batted her eyelashes at him. "You'll have to settle for my best attempt at an adoring look, I'm afraid."

He took a glance at her face and chuckled. "Looks more like indigestion to me. Shall we take a stroll on the veranda before supper?"

Their lighthearted banter set the tone for the evening, and George was amused to discover how many men gave him sly glances — and admiring ones. Harry, after one searching look at both of them, nodded and clearly accepted George's role with his sister was more important than helping him. In the end it worked for both causes, as several young ladies tried to coerce him away from Susannah. They didn't succeed but still, it gave Harry some respite from their attentions, and by the time George took his leave, he was in a better frame of mind than he had arrived in.

* * * *

His Sunday Bible reading at church was peacefully uneventful and on Monday morning, rested and fresh, he headed south towards Leyburn.

The ride on a clear warm day lifted his spirits even more. The weather was clement, the roads reasonable, and George skirted the major towns, preferring less frequented places. He met no one he knew, saw no young ladies being abducted and encountered no scoundrels or rogues.

Tame.

He couldn't help but compare this journey to the one on which he'd met Grace.

I wonder where her home is?

He supposed he could find out if he tried. However, he reminded himself as he halted and partook of a pie and a jug of ale in a very snug hostelry which reminded him of the inn where he'd first met Grace, to do so would break the rules of fair play. One night of love, agreed by both parties to never be mentioned again, had been their joint decision.

He had given her his word on the matter as a gentleman, so he couldn't in all honour invent an excuse to break it. An overture from the lady concerned would have been a different matter entirely. It would be perfectly acceptable for Grace to contact him if she were so inclined. And she knew where he lived, and also where Duncan and Cairstine resided. Didn't she?

George frowned as the seed of doubt took root and bloomed. He frequently mentioned his home at Back Blindburn in conversation, but had he done so during the time he'd spent in Grace's company? Had he actually named Duncan and Cairstine's house when they'd arrived there? He couldn't remember.

Water under the bridge. Time to move on, perhaps? Get a wife and an heir? The notion was so unappealing as to not merit further consideration, so he drained his tankard, settled up with the landlord and headed south once more.

* * * *

"'Tis a wonder that babe isn't full of herself and spoiled something terrible," Nettie McGovern, Grace's old nanny and now her companion, said as she watched the baby gurgle. "She's a charmer."

"Indeed she is." Grace laughed as her daughter blew a series of drool bubbles out of her mouth. "I am amazed how even-tempered she is. Everyone dotes on her and caters to her every whim. If a child of seven months old has such things."

Nettie sighed. "If only her papa could have lived to see her. Well made up he would be. How excited he must have been to discover he was to be a father after all this time."

Grace smiled noncommittally. She had heard not so much as a whisper concerning George since the day she had returned home. His name had been conspicuous by its absence in the society columns of the daily newspaper, and a polite enquiry as to whether she had arrived back safely, made say, through the offices of a mutual friend like Cairstine, had never arrived, no matter how longed for. The thought she had been dismissed so easily from George's mind still rankled, and also ensured the misconception over the paternity of her child must stand. Her baby's father had no idea he was a parent, and she had no line of communication through which to let him know it was so.

She lifted Georgina into her arms. "Time for a nap, little one. No, do not eat Mama's pearls. They would not digest." Georgina's face puckered up. "Come now, no need to cry. Nap, then we will go for a walk. Look for…"

She searched her mind for something to cheer both herself and her daughter, and the elderly Romany who wandered the area to the joy of all came to mind. "The man with the barrel organ. We can listen to the music and watch the monkey dance."

Grace generally disliked the thought of any animal, especially a wild animal, being used to entertain the populace, but at least the local organ grinder treated his monkey, rabbit, cat and dog with care.

Nettie beamed. "A good idea. I'll get on with some mending."

"Do you wish to come with us? We could stroll on The Stray and head into town for a mug of chocolate. Or," Grace added mischievously, "take the waters."

"No thank you." Nettie shuddered. "I don't care who says taking the waters does you good. Nasty stuff. It makes me bilious."

Grace nodded. "I agree with you, although many swear by it. If you truly don't want to come, Nettie, I'll take young Lily." The nursemaid enjoyed such trips. "She likes the walk."

"That she does. Younger limbs than mine. You go with Lily, and I'll do some sewing. Time our babe had a pinafore."

As she put the baby down for her nap, Grace lovingly traced the outline of the tiny heart-shaped birthmark on her infant's arm. "Oh, my love." Whether she was talking about the baby or her baby's father she wasn't sure. "He might not know you exist, but he would be as in love with you as I am."

For a while she sat by the cot watching as the tot sucked her thumb, closed her eyes and drifted off to sleep. If only all problems could be soothed by way of a short, blissful nap. Grace wandered around the nursery aimlessly. She was out of sorts and didn't know why.

She stared unseeing out of the window at the pleasant garden with its few fruit trees and flourishing vegetable plot.

How lucky this house was now hers. It was perfect for her and her loyal staff to continue living there when Roger had died and his distant cousin had taken over the estate. Fortuitously, Roger had known the type of man Thompson Foston was, and had put an unbreakable clause in his will that Foston Grange near

Harrogate, described as an imposing pile in a local guide, was to be hers and hers alone, to dispose of as she desired.

Thompson had ranted and raved, but the property was not entailed and in the end he'd had to accept the situation, albeit with a bad attitude. Grace had also been gifted a sizeable cash legacy, which meant she need not worry about her or her child's future.

Except for two important points.

No husband for her or father for her child.

It was galling, now she was out of mourning and permitted to rejoin society again, how many men thought that meant she would be happy to take up an offer of *carte blanch* then became unpleasant when she firmly thwarted their ideas and intentions. It had almost led to her staying as reclusive as she had been obliged to be for the previous year. If it hadn't been for Nettie, who had come out of what she called a dreary retirement and chivvied Grace into going out, Grace had a nasty feeling she might well have spent the rest of her life without enjoying it.

If only… How she hated thinking those two words. So many thoughts could begin with them, and end in, 'but not to be'. Far better to try to think positively.

If only I hadn't married Roger just because it was convenient. If only Jane could have just married Alfred. If only I hadn't met – She caught the thought before it fully formed.

Grace stood up and leaned over the crib as Lily entered the room.

"Oh, ma'am, I'm sorry I'm late up here. Um… I was sorting out what we'd need for our walk. Ah…I thought, perhaps, the little one might need a light blanket?"

Grace frowned at her nursemaid. This was not the first time she had been lax in her duties. Perhaps, Grace thought, she should share her concern with Nettie and see if she had noticed anything amiss. She doubted a query to Lily would bring forth any explanation. That young lady could be very mulish when challenged — even in a subtle or nonconfrontational way.

"Very good. Go and get everything together, and I'll bring her down with when she wakes. I doubt it will be long now."

Lily curtseyed. It was an accepted fact in the household that Grace did as much as she could for the baby and spent as much time with her as possible. Which was just as well, as Lily always seemed to find something to be busy with whilst Grace had her private time with her child.

Grace watched her go and returned her attention to her daughter, who began to stir. As she watched, Georgina opened her eyes, saw her mother and gave her a two-toothed gummy grin before waving her arms in the air.

The birthmark showed and Grace's heart missed a beat.

"Oh, Georgina, my little love. How like your papa you are. Would he love you as much as I do, I wonder?"

Would he even care? The women he usually consorts with are probably more worldly wise and know how to prevent such things.

She'd had no clue how to manage such matters. Her time with Roger hadn't brought any need for that information.

Grace wiped a tear from her eye and lifted her daughter from the cot. "Let's get you ready and we will go and find some fresh air."

* * * *

George rode into the yard of the Old Hall Inn just before dusk. Although it was several miles to the north of the market town of Leyburn, it was within easy reach of the estate where, if all went well, Sir William would sell him a dozen or so Dale of Goyt ewes George hoped would strengthen his own flock.

He was soon settled into his room and, over a tankard of porter, his mind returned to the subject that had been occupying him all day. Perhaps enough time had passed for it to be acceptable for him to seek out a little information with regards to Grace and her husband without the action breaking his promise to her? Just to reassure himself all was well. He sipped and cautioned himself. It would have to be done in such a way as not to draw attention to himself, or her.

She does not deserve conjecture or gossip. I just need to know she is happy.

He resolved to instruct McEwen to discreetly put matters in motion when he returned to Back Blindburn. Surely the current whereabouts of Roger Foston could be easily discovered? He need only tell McEwen there was a small matter he wished to discuss with Foston concerning his own father, Gordon. The request shouldn't raise any eyebrows. His father and Foston had been acquainted, after all. No one would be any the wiser about his true need to discover the man's whereabouts. With that resolution firmly in mind, George slept a good eight hours and woke up refreshed, to the crow of a nearby cockerel.

It was still early, the sun barely risen, and after a well-cooked breakfast George headed off. Sampson was saddled and waiting and the ostler gave directions for the best route to take. It was pleasant riding along in the warm September sunshine, and he soon discarded his greatcoat and strapped it to the back of his saddle. If all went well, he would arrange for his sheep — if they became his sheep — to travel to his home before winter set in. They would add nicely to his flock and, he hoped, improve the coffers of the estate.

George smiled to himself at the thought of the rams lining up to do their duty with multiple ewes. Thank goodness the human species didn't procreate in the same manner. Although he could think of a few of his over amorous peers who would relish the opportunity given the chance. So deep in his amusing thoughts did he become, he didn't realise he had wandered from the road onto a narrow, overgrown track until Sampson stopped walking with a snort.

What on earth?

George came out of his reverie, scanned his surroundings and swore under his breath. Nothing like the track he was now on had been mentioned when the ostler had given directions to his destination. He turned Sampson and retraced his route for about half a mile until he came to a crossroads with a lopsided signpost leaning drunkenly on a gate post.

Damn and blast. That is what comes of my not paying attention. However, even if he had been aware of the signpost, would the directions its wooden arms pointed to have been of any use?

Probably not. George peered at it and decided it would have been easier to translate Latin — a wretchedly archaic language that had never been his forte. Half the letters had worn off and the other half made no sense. With a muffled curse at whoever had carved the damn thing — why he muffled it he had no idea, there was no man nor beast around as far as the eye could see — *and* whoever had not maintained the signpost, he mentally tossed a coin and turned to the left.

Thirty minutes later he muttered something very uncomplimentary under his breath and set off cross-country towards a building he spied a mile or so in the distance. With a bit of luck someone there would be able to point him in the right direction. He was disappointed when he reached it and saw it was a sadly half-derelict barn with a crumbling roof.

The sky became progressively darker. Thunder rumbled and a crack of lightning caused Sampson to rear up and shy. It even made George jump, and he wasn't usually worried about storms. However, this time he was at one with Sampson. It was too close for comfort. He soothed Sampson as best he could, and as the rain came down heavily, urged him into the portion of the barn that still offered shelter.

It was not at all comfortable but at least they would be reasonably dry. He dismounted, loosened Sampson's girth and tied him to a ring obviously there for the purpose. It wasn't a proper stall as such, but there was a hay net — half-full — and a bucket of water that was reasonably clean and sweet smelling.

With swift, economical movements, George dried his stallion down with a whisp of hay, then tried to do the same for himself by using his half-sodden cravat. What he must look like he could only guess, but more than likely not in the sort of state in which he'd want to meet Sir William.

Cursing the fact he'd not had time to don his greatcoat before the heavens had opened, he sat on an upturned wheelbarrow and contemplated his next move. A change of clothes was available in his saddlebag, but he would not put them on and leave the barn until the weather improved or, greatcoat or no, he'd soon be soaked through again. He stood when a male voice interrupted his train of thought.

"Steady there, little lady. Shelter is at hand."

The rider checked his horse then stared at George, who took a step forward so as to be seen with ease.

"My apologies." George put his hands out in an 'I am unarmed and no threat' gesture as a rider edged his honey-coloured mare in through the aperture. "I mean no trespass, but I was caught by the storm and took shelter until the worst passes." He smiled ruefully. "If it ever does. I was on my way to visit Sir William Drake with a view to purchasing a few of his flock, but this weather appears set for the night."

The man dismounted. "I'm afraid you're heading in the wrong direction. Sir William lives on the other side of Leyburn. If you set off now you'd arrive too late for him to receive you. He keeps *very* country hours, and has a reputation for, shall we say, ah, eccentricity. Metaphorically pulls the drawbridge up at six or dusk—whichever is earlier."

By the man's tone he did not appear overly enamoured of the peer, but something else about his voice poked George's memory. He took a second look, then smiled. "Major Winterbottom?"

The other man started then flashed George a smile. "Baron Renfrew? Well, I never."

George held out his hand. "The very same. Well met, sir."

His hand was heartily shaken. "If it's Dale of Goyt sheep you're after, Jane and I also breed them, and I

swear every one of them is as good as any in his flock."
He winked. "If not better."

"They are for sale?" George hadn't had a hint of
another breeder willing to sell, other than Sir William —
if he could be called willing. *Willing William. Ha!* "I
didn't know of any other breeder who had any to sell."

"Normally not, we are just building up our flock.
But to you, my lord? Of course. Make a dash with me
when the thunder rolls over? Jane would be more than
happy to put you up for the night, then you can view
them on the morrow."

* * * *

It was an offer George was happy to accept, as were
the roaring fire and glass of brandy he was given after
Major Winterbottom escorted him inside a four-square
manor house. He swirled the spirit around the bottom
of his glass and hoped Mrs Winterbottom would bring
up the most absorbing subject in his life. Her sister,
Grace.

Jane sipped her ratafia. "I am happy to see you, my
lord. It has been quite some while since we met, and
times have moved on for us. You must be surprised to
find us living near Leyburn but Major Winterbottom is
now Major Winterbottom, Retired."

"You have resigned your commission, sir?" George
asked. "I never imagined that would be the case for
you. I thought you happy in the army."

"I was, but it was time to move on." Major
Winterbottom smiled contentedly. "The life of a
gentleman farmer is to be preferred now my wife and I
are expecting a happy event."

Jane blushed. "Alfred. You shouldn't say yet. I have another four months to go."

He chuckled. "Maybe or maybe not. Your sister's babe was born a little ahead of time, so who knows, the same may happen to you too."

George swallowed hard. *No!*

His hand shaking slightly, he forced himself to ask. "Grace has a child? Her husband must be delighted."

Jane sighed. "Unfortunately, we have no idea. Poor Roger passed away before he even knew Grace was *enceinte*. It's been the talk of Harrogate how he must have rallied before the end."

Major Winterbottom laughed. "And gossip also has it that it must have been all the excitement of the act of union that sent him on his way."

Harrogate. How long will it take me to get there? Would she want me to?

George's hand trembled with the news, and he set his glass onto the table. It rattled and he took a deep breath. "I must send my felicitations."

The cuff of his shirt rode up as he did so, and Jane stared at it keenly.

"How very strange. My niece, Grace's babe, has a heart-shaped birthmark just like yours on her upper arm."

George didn't need a mirror to tell him the colour had just drained out of his face. Jane bit her lip but didn't comment on his reaction. "Georgina's such a sweet child. She's about seven months old now. Perhaps you could visit if you're ever in the Harrogate vicinity…?"

George steadied himself, calculated the distance across country versus stamina of his powerful stallion, then picked up his brandy. "With luck, I shall be in the vicinity by this time tomorrow. Harrogate, you say?"

Major Winterbottom toasted him with his glass. "Jane will pinpoint her address on the map for you, and I will inform Sir William you have unexpectedly been called away on business so will not be viewing his flock."

George knocked back his brandy in one short gulp. "Thank you."

* * * *

Georgina was mightily amused by both the antics of the monkey and the music until the storm clouds rolled in and forced them to return home. Lily held the baby close to her and they picked up the pace as the first drops of rain fell. Safely indoors with only a sprinkling on each of their heads, Grace's relief was short-lived when she saw the Reverend Sample waiting for her in the hall.

He jumped to his feet. "Now, when are you getting this babe christened?" The reverend was rotund, with cheeks as rosy as a russet apple and hair as white as the proverbial freshly fallen snow, but his looks belied his determination. "She is more than old enough."

'Too old', his tone inferred. He pinched the baby's cheek. "Isn't that right, my sweet little child?"

Georgina, predictably, shied away and Grace sighed. How could she explain it didn't seem right to hold such a public occasion when her beloved daughter's father knew nothing about her? During the service she might be asked to confirm the father's name, and she would not lie in church. She looked at her nursemaid, who was standing in the corner gazing abstractedly into the far distance. "Lily, take Georgina upstairs to Nanny Nettie, please. It's beyond time she was fed."

Lily jumped as if startled, then complied, and Grace returned her attention to the reverend to continue the same unceasing conversation they'd been having for the last several months. "She *will* be baptized but…not yet."

It was the vicar's turn to sigh. "Very well. I will, of course, accede to your wishes, but also be warned I will not stop reminding you this child needs to become part of the Church."

"One day," Grace promised. *Perhaps when she can speak for herself.*

"And with that," the vicar said, eyeing her sadly, "I suppose I will have to be satisfied."

"I'm afraid so." Grace watched him walk briskly down the drive and wondered not for the first time where George was and what he was doing. Anyone who saw him and Georgina together would not be able to miss the likeness. It wasn't obvious at first glance, but then… The stubborn chin, the intense scrutiny Georgina gave people, the eyes, the —

Enough.

Nevertheless, once seated with the tea tray in the parlour, she still couldn't get George out of her mind. Had he returned to his home in the north? The absence of gossip in the papers proved nothing. Was he once more in the capital and living the life of a well-to-do single man? The thought didn't sit well with her.

He might be single but he's mine!

However, if that were the case, now her period of mourning was over, why hadn't she at least have tried to communicate with him? To say she didn't know his direction was a feeble excuse. She could have found out if she had wanted to. Why had she dithered? Deep down she knew the reason. In case she'd mistaken George's feelings, and he rejected her.

Excuses, excuses...

She sat straighter. It was time to move forward. She didn't think George had viewed her as someone to dally with then promptly forget, but she would never be able to settle until she knew the truth of the matter, one way or the other. She hurried into the study.

First, she had to try to remember where she had met Duncan and Cairstine then wrack her brains as to whether George had ever mentioned his home. She opened a drawer and pulled out a book — *Maps of England Wales and Scotland.*

* * * *

The following morning, she was not a lot further forward in her search. She could pinpoint the rough location of Duncan and Cairstine's house from the terrain she had travelled on horseback, but the house was not actually named on the map. A book detailing the history of the area should provide the required information, and to find such a thing, an outing to a library more extensive than her own would be needed, she decided.

Her near neighbour Lady Donnington possessed just such a thing, so she took a piece of scented notepaper from the drawer and began to compose a short enquiry as to when would be a convenient time to visit. Nanny Nettie opened the door as she laid the quill down and sanded the paper.

Grace looked up. "Will you be so kind as to give this to the hall boy to take round, Nettie?"

Nettie took the note then frowned. "I will do. Ah... I wondered if you've noticed anything amiss with Lily lately?"

"As in?" Grace realized she'd not brought the subject up earlier as she had meant to. "I had intended to ask you that very question, but it slipped my mind."

"Like her being more dreamy than usual. Yesterday she dressed Georgina in odd socks and this morning she disappeared to goodness knows where when she should have been absent from the nursery for no longer than it takes to run downstairs and warm the baby's weaning pap."

Grace nodded. "She is not her usual helpful self. She gazes, daydreaming, instead of paying attention to her job. But then, bless her, she is not the most...intelligent of people, shall we say. Somewhat slow on the uptake at times. Perhaps she has eyes for the butcher's boy. He has rather a reputation for turning young girl's heads, I believe. But as long as she continues to attend willingly to Lily's needs..."

"Not so much willing these days." Nettie tutted and shook her head. "As you say, probably hankering after some youth. I noticed her looking sheep's eyes at young Ernest down at the farm the other day as well. She's always talking about the perfect man who will, one day, sweep her off her feet."

"Well, the butcher's boy is most certainly not the one for her then. With his cheeky winks at all and sundry, if he was female, I'd call him flighty. Nor is young Ernest. He's more likely tell her to get out of the way so he can tend to the animals." Grace thought of her own youthful romantic yearnings. "Best advise Lily to keep her feet firmly on the ground. Such grand gestures only happen in fairy tales."

Nettie nodded. "I'll keep an eye on her. Make sure any intentions towards her are honourable, or I'll see to it they're nipped them in the bud. Too daft, her, to know what's real or not. All fairy-tale endings in her mind, nothing to do with the practicalities of life as we know it."

The long case clock in the hall struck a half hour, and Nettie jumped. "Lawks, look at the time. I best get on. I promised Cook I'd check the stew. She's never sure about the seasoning." She bustled out.

Grace nodded, amused at how easily Nettie could change a subject. Lily might be feather-brained, but she was also good-natured, and Georgina adored her. Grace would be loath to lose the services of her nursemaid. She glanced out of the window and saw the pair of them taking the air in the garden — Georgina laid on a rug while Lily amused her by shaking a rattle. Oh, to be outside!

Why not?

She didn't resist for more than a minute and left the study to join them.

Pippin, the kitchen cat, lazed in the shade of a tree nearby, and Grace smiled at the sight of her feeding the three kittens Grace had refused to be allowed to be drowned. The cook had argued they were surplus to requirements. Grace had disagreed.

"*We'll be overrun,*" Cook had huffed. "*Someone'll have to feed them. Look after 'em.*" And it wouldn't be her, her tone had intimated.

"*So be it,*" Grace had replied firmly.

Cook's attitude hadn't lasted long, and within days Grace had caught her crooning to them and putting out dishes of leftover scraps where Pippin and the kittens could find them. It probably did make the household cat numbers too high, but for once Grace didn't care. It was her house, her home, her rules.

She smiled to herself as she continued to make her way across the lawn. Life was good —

In the next instant there was a screech of alarm. Grace turned to see Lily pick up Georgina and dart across the lawn. One kitten, more daring than the others, had escaped the critical gaze of its mama and was climbing the trunk of the tree. It reached the first overhanging branch then the second before it realised what it had done and began to mewl.

"I'll get him. Stay clear with the baby." Grace ran over, grasped the branch and swung herself upward to sit on it. "There now," she crooned to the frightened kitten. "Just let me get you, and we'll be on the ground in a jiffy." She considered her options, slid a foot or two nearer to the terrified animal and did her best to ignore its pitiful yowls. From her new position it was not a far stretch to lift the kitten and jump down with it in her arms.

"Oh, madam. You are brave," Lily gasped as Grace set the small creature on the ground. "I was right scared."

Grace smoothed her skirts. Hoofbeats crunched on gravel, and Grace peered around the tree trunk to see who had arrived and could hardly believe her eyes.

George!

There right in front of her. Riding up her drive as if he didn't have a care in the world. After all this time. Without one single word from him. *How dare he?* She glared and fought the urge to tap her foot. What to do for the best? She didn't want to meet him here, windswept and sweaty. She needed to get back to the house unseen and tidy up a bit. "Lily, take Georgina back to the nursery. I believe I'm about to find out just how brave I can be."

Chapter Seven

George took a deep breath when he arrived at the gates to Foston Grange. Jane's directions had been spot-on. He turned Sampson to go up the drive and, unsure of his welcome, proceeded at no more than a gentle trot. His card was accepted when he presented it at the front door though, and ten minutes later his heart missed a beat when he was shown into a sunny parlour and saw Grace perched on a fireside chair. He stuttered her name and saw, beneath her skirt, her foot start to tap on the floor.

"Well, my lord? To what do I owe this honour?"

That is not a welcoming voice.

All his rehearsed sentences dried in his throat, leaving only his heartfelt plea. "Grace...don't be like that. Please?"

The tattoo on the polished wooden surface beneath her feet beat faster. "Like what...?"

He shut his eyes for a brief moment and decided to be honest. Say how he felt. "Stand-offish... As if there's nothing between us."

"My lord." Grace's voice was cold. "I've heard neither hide nor hair of you in well over a year. What on earth could there be between us after such a period of time?" Her eyes flashed. "Anything could have happened to either of us!"

Was it anger or hurt he saw? If the latter, he knew the cause and hurried to explain himself. "My love, in the last few days I have, by the merest chance, seen Jane. Why didn't you send word to tell me? I'd have been here long before now if you had."

Grace stiffened. "When I returned home I thought, maybe hoped to receive, let's say from Cairstine perhaps, a note asking if I'd arrived home safely. I heard nothing. What reason did I have not to presume that to you I was a casual liaison?"

George walked closer and tipped up her chin with his fingertips. "Because you know deep down it was never like that for either of us."

"I was alone and pregnant with our child," she said flatly. "And when I didn't receive so much as a polite enquiry, afraid you would reject us."

He swallowed hard. "All I could think was that you were legally bound to another and there was no hope... I made you a promise. The only way I could keep it was to stay out of your life. You must understand that."

She bit down on his finger, hard. "Oh, must I?"

"Ouch!" He pulled his hand away. "Hellcat!"

"Rake!" Grace shot back.

The familiarity of their exchange lifted his spirits so he gazed into her eyes and prayed his words wouldn't be inadequate. That they would be enough to convey the depth of the emotions he felt. "My heart longed for you so much, but my head was telling me I must ignore those feelings. They would only prolong the pain of our not being able to be together. I had made a promise not to come between you and your husband, so I forced myself not to try and discover where you lived. How you were. It was hell on earth…but I told myself it was for the best." Did her expression soften? George prayed it had. "I'm sorry, sweetheart. I would give anything to have been with you for the birth of our child. There's never been anyone but you since the night we made love. I promise."

Her lip trembled, and more so when he added huskily, "Can I see her? Our baby. Georgina."

He thought she might refuse when she turned her head away, but then, with what he suspected was a surreptitious sniffle covered by a small cough, she held out her hand. "Come along. I'll take you to the nursery."

Grace opened the door to a sun-filled room, and he caught the first sight of his daughter. The babe was propped up in her bassinet with a pillow behind her back. Her nursemaid stopped crooning the rhyme she was singing and bobbed a curtsey. "Shall I run down to the kitchen and prepare her pap boat if you're here to mind her for a while, madam?"

Grace nodded. The baby was ready for her milk-soaked bread weaning feed. "If you would. Thank you, Lily." George walked over to the bassinet as the maid left the room and stroked his finger down Georgina's cheek. She wrapped a plump fist around it and pulled it to her mouth.

"Just like your mother." He chuckled. "What is it with the women in my life that as soon as they see me, they feel the need to bite me?"

Georgina gurgled her gummy happiness at his teasing tone, and Grace smiled. "She's cutting her milk teeth."

George reached for his daughter. "Can I hold her?"

"Be warned, you'll have a cravat soaked in dribble if you do."

He scooped up the warm bundle of wriggling lace-clad babe and kissed the soft dark hair on her head. The distinctive birthmark at the top of her arm marked Georgina as his, but even without it, the shape of her eyes and the little cleft in the centre of her chin would have told him this was so.

My child. My daughter. Ours!

Who would have thought it a mere couple of days previous? That he would be holding his babe, standing beside the woman he adored. He thought his heart would burst with the love that filled it. He shifted Georgina into one arm, her head on his shoulder, slipped the other around Grace's waist and urged her closer. "She's beautiful, my love. I might have missed the first months of her life, but I will not be missing any more of them unless it is by your choice. My days have been long and cold without you. No more missing you, and you me, I hope." He waited for her reply with bated breath. *What if she said it* was *her choice he went away?*

Grace did not resist his touch, and to his relief moved under the shelter of his arm.

"Oh, do you? Well, we shall see. You have some making up to do on that front, my lord." Her tone was light and teasing.

The scent of her filled his nose. She slipped her hand around his back and rested it on his left buttock.

His nether regions stirred. "Are you flirting with me, madam?"

The door handle clicked and with a cheeky pinch on his rear Grace took a step away. "That is for you to discover, my lord."

The door opened and a stout, grey-haired lady walked through it carrying a spouted ceramic dish filled with milky gruel. Grace frowned. "Where is Lily, Nettie? She was meant to be fetching Georgina's pap."

"The dratted girl's gone a-wandering again. I found the task half-done, so finished it. I shall give her what-for when she turns up again."

George did not envy the nursemaid's next encounter with the old lady, from the fierce look on her face. Grace introduced them. "This lovely lady was mine and Jane's, and is now Georgina's, nanny, Nettie.

"Nettie, this is Lord Renfrew. A dear friend of mine."

The lady bustled forward and took Georgina from him. George nearly chuckled when, with a piercing stare at his face, she snorted. "So, I see."

Grace's eyes sparkled with mirth as Nettie sat on the low nursing chair to feed Georgina. Thankfully, Grace seemed of a like mind to him in that a hasty retreat was in order. "How remiss of me, my lord. I have not yet offered you any refreshment after your journey to visit us. Please come this way."

He followed her from the room, and they let out their laughter on the landing once he'd shut the door behind them. "Oh my." Grace giggled, the beauty of her features alight with her smile. He couldn't wait a moment longer to hold her, so put his hands on her waist, lifted, and threw her over his shoulder. "You promised me refreshment, I believe."

Her much-smaller-than-his fists beat on his back, although her giggles did not stop. "George Armstrong, this is outrageous! Put me down at once."

He smacked her bottom. "Not a chance of it, woman. Our daughter will require a brother or two, and perhaps a couple more sisters. Practice will be needed. Lots of it."

Grace seemed to like the idea too, as although she gasped at the sting of his palm, she then slapped his own arse and laughed. "One floor down, you wretch. Second door along the hall and hurry up. I can't hang around upside down like this all day, you know."

George needed no second urging and set off at a fast walk, only encountering one startled housemaid on his way when, with his hands full, he kicked the door open. He deposited his fair burden on a beautifully carved-in-the-French-style bed, then walked back to the door and turned the key in the lock against well-meaning intruders while shrugging off his jacket. His somewhat soggy cravat he discarded as he turned and saw Grace's urgency matched his own.

Her dress hit the floor in a crumpled heap as he gazed into her eyes and walked closer, unfastening the neck of his shirt. She locked her eyes on his and released the buttons on the front of her chemise. His breath caught when the round moons of her full breasts appeared.

Grace's voice dropped to a purr. "Take it all off. Let me see you. Every inch of you. Naked."

His cock threatened to burst from his breeches, and slowly, as instructed, he stripped. She ran the tip of tongue over her top lip as she watched him do so then she pulled off her chemise and threw it to the side of the bed. Only her gartered stockings remained, and as his gaze fastened on the golden triangle between her legs, she parted them. "Take me...?"

With a low growl in the back of his throat he launched himself forward, lay over her and claimed her mouth for his own. Their tongues meshed, and she returned his kiss with equal passion. The vein along the length of his shaft throbbed. He moved his head and fastened his mouth onto the pert nipple pressed against his chest, and she moaned. "Yes, George. More...more..."

He plucked and pulled her other nipple with his fingertips while tugging on the first with his teeth. Grace writhed beneath him. "Now...please...please."

He could wait no longer either so stroked the sweet, wet place between her legs and plunged his cock in. Her back arched, and she wrapped her legs around his thighs. "Yes... Yes..."

They matched each other thrust for thrust until Grace stiffened, knotted her fingers through the back of his hair and mewled, "Oh, sweet Jesus, yessss..."

His climax arrived seconds behind hers. "Oh God."

They clung together, breathing hard. George whispered small kisses along Grace's neck. "My sweet love. So perfect..."

They lay entwined for some time until Grace stirred. "Goodness, I must re-dress. The household will be wondering just where I've disappeared to at this time of the day."

George smiled and kissed the top of her head. "I believe they may know by now, my love. The rather inconvenient housemaid on the stairs will have informed them."

* * * *

Grace steeled herself for the inevitable scandalized whisperings between the staff, but they faded over the next few days when the household realised Baron Renfrew was no passing visitor, but Mrs Foston's soon-to-be husband and, therefore, their future master.

Likewise, two days later, when she and George pushed Georgina to the rectory in her new wheeled bassinet, Reverend Sample's frowns at the hastiness of their request for the banns of marriage to be called without delay disappeared once George spoke to him

"Of course, following the formalization of our union, my wife and I shall take the legal steps necessary to change Georgina's surname to Armstrong," he told the man. "Henceforth I will be her father and she, my daughter."

"And the matter of her baptism, my lord?"

"Shall be completed on the first Sunday after I receive the signed and sealed court papers containing the testament to her name change, if it would be convenient to yourself to conduct the service with such short notice?"

The reverend's expression became positively benign as he beamed and offered out his hand. "To be sure, it will. Please allow me to my welcome you to my flock, my lord. You will be an asset and an example to all, I'm sure. Well…once the county has got over the irregularity of your arrival here with us, I expect."

Grace nearly laughed out loud and, unseen by the vicar, slyly pinched George's arm. So in tune had they become, he immediately understood her silent message and excused them once he had shaken the reverend's hand. "I thank you for your welcome, sir. Come, my love. It's a beautiful day. We should give Georgina the benefit of a little additional fresh air."

Grace smiled her acquiescence and pushed the wheeled baby carriage from the room. George bowed and followed her out. His façade cracked as they strolled down the lane back to Foston House, and he grinned. "It is as well my previous reputation never made its way to his ears, then. Added to the rest, he would probably decide we are both reprobates of the first order and refuse to marry us out of hand."

Grace gave him a rueful smile. "Let us hope our intention to sell Foston Grange and move to Corbridge once the legalities are complete does not escape by way of the lawyer's office and become common knowledge. Reverend Sample might just change his mind."

"Hence the haste. The shorter the time the formalities take to complete, the less the likelihood of our having to appeal to the bishop for a special licence and avoid all the additional gossip that would then ensue."

"The sooner the better then," Grace agreed fervently.

They strolled on, the perfect picture of a respectable couple — a stance they were careful to maintain as their wedding day approached. They ate their dinner each evening with perfect propriety then retired to their respective rooms until the household quietened down. Only then would George pad silently to Grace's bedroom so they could make sweet love for an hour or so before they parted once more.

* * * *

Two days before Reverend Sample was due to make them man and wife, Jane and Alfred were to arrive at Foston Grange to witness the wedding and give them the same countenance Grace herself had provided for Jane. No other guests were to be invited. The less wagging tongues the better, they'd decided. With George's father, Gordon, as a prime example of how gossip, warranted or not, lingered for years, neither wished to risk Georgina's future prospects by having parents who were considered by society in general to be 'not up to snuff'.

George kissed Grace's lips before he left her. "I cannot wait for this subterfuge to be over, sweetheart. I long to fall asleep with you in my arms and wake with you in the morning without having to steal away to my own cold bed."

Grace stroked her fingertips down his cheek. "Not long now, my love. Jane's and Alfred's company will be a boon. The time will pass before we know it. You and Alfred will talk Goyt sheep, pastures, ewes and lambs for hours, while Jane will have much she wishes to discuss with me in regard to her upcoming confinement. I best gloss over some of the more, ah, shall we say, *gory* details and promote the joy of the end result. Sing the benefits of mutton broth, a warm salt bath and the love of a good man. Not necessarily in that order."

"Domesticity at its finest." George smiled. "Which, as you surmise, I shall enjoy very much."

Grace turned her cheek to the pillow when the door clicked softly shut behind him. She was looking forward to spending time with her sister. She and Jane had been each other's constant support through the unpleasant years of living under their stepmother's rule, and each of them desired only the happiness of the other. She had hers and was sure Jane did also. The child due soon would cement the felicity of her sister's marriage to Alfred, Grace was sure.

* * * *

The morning dawned fair and warm. Nothing about it hinted that, even given Jane's condition, their journey could not be undertaken—and so it proved.

Midway through the afternoon the kerfuffle of visitors arriving sounded. Raised voices could be heard, laughter, then the stentorian toes of her major-domo replying to someone.

Grace smiled at George, leapt to her feet and rushed from the parlour into the hall to greet them. Alfred escorted Jane in through the front door, and even in civilian clothing his compact body and upright, square-shouldered stance marked him as a military man, retired though he might be. Her sister's swelling belly was largely concealed by the drapery of her dress, but Grace could see the difference in her outline and urged her in to take the weight from her feet.

"Jane, you are here! Come, our most comfortable armchair awaits you in the parlour. A light repast will be served to you directly. It is nothing heavy. Just some small savoury tartlets, honeyed cakes and fresh fruit to see you through to dinner."

"I am fine," Jane protested as Grace kissed her cheek. "A little weary, but whenever is one not after sitting in a carriage for several hours? I swear I wonder every time how being idle makes you tired."

Grace laughed. "I agree. But still come and rest in a comfortable chair, not a swaying carriage."

Alfred, his moustache as luxuriously fine as ever, smiled. "You have borne the journey very well, my love. Go with your sister and take your ease."

George walked forward and held out his hand. "Welcome, and may I offer you something a little more reviving in the library, sir?"

Alfred's eyes twinkled as he shook it. "Indeed, you may, my lord. With my heartfelt thanks."

Grace took Jane by the hand and led her to the parlour. The men turned away and headed towards the dining room. Jane's bonnet was soon removed, and Grace slid a footstool under her feet. Her sister relaxed back into her chair with a small sigh. "I would not miss this occasion for all the world, but I must admit, the journey has tired me — but I'm only six months along so will soon recover with a light repast, and dare I say it given the time of day, a cup of tea?"

Grace smiled and rang the bell. "I'm sure Nanny Nettie would hustle you off to bed, but as it is her day off you may drink your tea in peace."

Jane sat straighter and perked up a little. "How is she? Who looks after the babe when she's not here?"

The topic, as Grace had hoped, diverted her sister's mind from the weariness of her travels. "Nettie is in fine form, and I have a nursemaid, Lily. Do you wish for Nanny to come to you when your time is due? Georgina will be nigh on a year old by then, and I think your need will be greater than mine."

Jane declaimed. Alfred's own nanny had promised to attend them — then once started on the subject that most nearly concerned her, she chatted on. How Alfred rubbed her back when it ached, massaged her feet when she was weary, fetched her the little delicacies that sometimes took her fancy…

Grace was happy her sister had comfort and support at the time she needed it most but found herself having to resolutely squash memories of her own loneliness whilst in the same condition. She was somewhat relieved when Jane changed the subject.

"You have not invited Papa to your wedding?" Jane asked.

Grace shrugged. "I haven't seen him, and neither has he written to me in an age. Has he even been home of late?"

Jane blushed. "It's probably because we live not so far from him and Stepmama, but yes. He called when passing two weeks ago. I had not long received your letter and invitation."

Grace shook her head. "Do not colour up because you have seen our father and I have not. Rather, it should be he who blushes with shame for the treatment he has meted out to us. I take it you told him?"

Her sister's eyes filled with tears. "Should I have not?"

With a rueful smile, Grace shrugged again. "It is probably of no matter other than now our stepmother will know."

"What harm can she do? She is nothing to us anymore."

"Not a lot, other than through sheer spite she will not have a good word to say about it..." She squeezed Jane's hand. "But as you say, she is of no consequence anymore. Let's dismiss her from our thoughts and concentrate on happier matters. Have you decided on any names?"

"We thought Alfreda for a girl, and Frederick for a boy."

Grace laughed. "A portion of Alfred's name in each. How clever of you. What about Frederica?"

Jane shuddered. "After the antics of that awful girl who attended Miss Botts Seminary For Young Ladies with us? The one who stole everyone's stockings and never admitted it? I think not."

"You have a point."

Colewell entered the room and announced dinner was served. They joined the men and, when the meal was complete, George planted a chaste kiss on her cheek.

"Until tomorrow."

Grace nodded and followed Jane up the stairs where they parted, each to their own room.

The oil lamp had been lit in her room, bathing it in a golden glow. She walked to her dressing table to let down her hair, noticed a cut crystal tumbler set upon it so picked it up, sniffed and smiled.

Glen Eyevie.

George was so thoughtful. They had not spent many minutes in each other's company today, but still he must have found a few moments to slip away and leave it for her. She sipped and the fiery liquid hit the back of her throat. Strong and peaty. She finished the glass as she undressed then settled beneath the covers, her eyelids feeling too heavy to stay open for even another minute.

It's been a busy day…

* * * *

The subject of sheep and everything to do with them having been exhausted for one day, George bid his guest goodnight on the landing and entered his solitary bedroom.

Just two more nights and I will no longer sleep alone.

A crystal tumbler set on the washstand made him smile. He picked it up and sniffed.

Glen Eyevie. Grace…you sweetheart.

He sipped while he undressed, then slipped into bed after he'd drained the glass, remembering the first time they'd drank it together.

The inn. A glass in my room. A glass after you hid in the tree.

Contented tiredness crept over him. He should go and take a peek at Georgina. He normally did on his nocturnal way to spend an hour with —

His eyelids closed on the thought.

* * * *

George struggled from the black depths. Why did he feel so sleepy? So…so…headachy and sick? He glanced around the room — his own, not Grace's.

Oh Lord, just how much did Alfred and I drink?

He looked at the whisky glass on the side table beside the bed and memory returned, hazy but true.

I was sober enough when I entered my room and saw it.

He put his feet to the floor and the room swam before his eyes.

Damn!

Gritting his teeth, he struggled upright and over to the washstand. A jug of washing water, now cold, stood beside the porcelain bow, and leaning forward he picked it up and poured over his head. His vision cleared. He gripped the washstand and breathed deep until he could stand upright and towel himself dry.

The house was quiet. Too quiet? He glanced at the timepiece on the mantel. It wanted but five minutes to seven o'clock. Early enough, but still he would have expected to hear faint footsteps running up and down the stairs as the maids prepared Georgina for her day and brought her feed to her. The only thing he could hear though was the steady tick of the clock.

He dressed quickly, not bothering to ring for a fresh jug of hot water in which to wash. His chin was grizzly with its normal overnight growth. He should not appear outside his room thus, but with a small nugget of apprehension building in his belly, decided his shave would have to wait. Firstly he would tap on Grace's door and wish her good morning, then a visit the nursery would be in order. He needed to reassure himself his daughter's needs were being taken care of.

* * * *

Grace woke, put her feet to the floor, swayed and grabbed hold of the bedpost to steady herself. A fuzzy-headedness and dry throat were like nothing she'd ever experienced before. Not even when she had been pregnant with Georgina.

Pregnant?

Of course, she *could* be, but common sense reasserted itself. If she were she would not be feeling anything yet.

Pregnant.

The thought gave her a warm glow inside. If she were lucky enough to be with child again, this time she would have George with her.

George.

He hadn't slipped into her room last night, but his not doing so was largely inevitable with visitors in the house. He and Alfred must have sat up and finished their bottle of port, as men often did once the ladies retired to bed. She hoped he was feeling somewhat better than she herself was this morning.

A few minutes sat quietly on the side of the bed cleared the mussiness from her head, allowing her then to complete her brief ablutions. She would order the tub to her room during the dressing hour before dinner — her hair required washing so as to be fresh for her wedding day. Her plain day gown fastened by way of small buttons at the side and did not require the assistance of a maid. Neither did the soft house shoes she slipped onto her feet.

The mantel clock chimed the quarter hour after seven as she pinned up her hair. Georgina would be taking her morning feed. She would run up to the nursery and dress her daughter herself and allow Lily to return below stairs to eat her own breakfast.

* * * *

George tapped softly on Grace's bedroom door, and her muffled voice answered, "Come in."

He cracked the door open a few inches. "Good morning, my love. It occurs to me I've heard little activity upstairs. I think I'll visit Georgina before breakfast."

She frowned. "Now you come to mention it, you're right. I would have more usually heard Georgina's demands for her pap before now. Wait for me. I'll come with you."

He pushed the door wider for her to pass through, and they walked up the stairs, the silence becoming more ominous with each flight. George flung the door to the nursery open then spluttered. "What the hell?"

Lily was laid flat on the floor, trussed up like the proverbial turkey, a handkerchief shoved into her mouth. Of Georgina there was no sign. Just an empty crib.

Grace issued a mewl of distress and darted forward. "Where is she? My baby. Where has she gone?"

George strode over to Lily, pulled the linen from her mouth and asked the same set of questions. Lily burst into noisy tears. "It weren't my fault. It were 'is."

Unease gnawing at his gut, George pulled at the knots binding the nursemaid's legs. "His? A man? Do you know him, Lily?"

The sobs became louder, and Lily's words more incoherent as she sat up and mucus ran from her nose. "Aid... Den... Cor..."

Grace picked up the handkerchief and thrust it at the maid as George released her hands. "Stop your bawling or I will slap you. Now, blow your nose. We have no time to stand here while you have hysterics."

Grace's harsh words had the desired effect. The sobs stopped. Lily hiccupped and sniffed, then did as requested.

George questioned her a little more gently. They needed the full circumstances surrounding Georgina's disappearance. Missing details could lead to a wild goose chase down the wrong path. "What happened last night, Lily? Tell us everything from the start. Leave nothing out."

Lily wiped the last of the mucus away and began. "It were all Ernest's fault really. If 'e 'adn't been leading me on I'd never 'ave done it... But I thought 'e loved me, so wiv Nanny not 'ere an' the baby sleeping, Polly said she would watch 'er while I slipped out fer a while..."

A tear trickled down her cheek. "But when I gotta the farm I see Ern kissing that milkmaid, Hannah, so I ran away home…"

The tears fell faster and Lily dabbed them with the screwed-up ball of sodden linen square. "I was pretty upset when I met 'im as I turned into our street. A right toff, but he were ever so nice. Stopped me, he did, an' asked why such a pretty maid as me was crying. He even gave me his own 'ankie."

George looked at the quality of the crumpled handkerchief Lily held. "That one?"

"Thas right."

He eased it from her hand and shook the revolting object to straighten it. The legend *A.C.* embroidered on one corner of it became apparent as he did so.

Grace gasped. "Corbett!"

Lily shook her head. "No, madam. *Corby.* Aiden Corby is what 'e said."

George gritted his teeth. "And he knew you were a maid. Did he also happen to know at which house you worked?"

Lily gazed at him round-eyed as if amazed at his acumen. "'E did, my lord. Said 'e was to be a guest at your wedding. That 'e was bringing you a special gift and how it was lucky as he'd bumped into me, 'cos now I could deliver it as a surprise…an' he'd give me a whole golden guinea if I did it proper."

Grace's foot began to tap upon the floor. "And just what was this special gift?"

"He gave me a bottle, ma'am. Said the contents were precious, real expensive, like what the king 'imself would drink. I was to pour each of you a big glassful in one of the posh glasses from the dining room and leave the drinks in your rooms. A nightcap 'e called it, but not like the ones yer wear on yer 'ead. He said as you would be proper made up to see it there waiting fer yer..."

Grace clutched his arm and interjected. "The whisky was drugged. But why would he choose Glen Eyvie, George?"

"Because he saw it in my room at the inn when he fell in through the door, I should think. I re-placed the bottle onto the dresser, but it had obviously been opened and poured from. He knew at least one of us was partial to it." He returned his attention to Lily and urged her on. "And then?"

"When everyone was asleep, I was to put a lamp in my window an' wait. He would hoot like an owl, then once I'd spotted 'im, I was to run downstairs to give 'im back the bottle, an' 'e would give me my guinea."

Grace shook her head sadly. "But he didn't, did he?"

Lily sniffed. "No, madam. When I opened the window an' see 'im outside 'e asked, was I wiv the baby, an' when I said yes, 'cos I was, what with Nanny Nettie not being 'ere, 'e said yer can't leave 'er. Was there a door open anywhere so 'e could come to me instead?"

"So you told him about the back stairs from the garden the maids use to bring coal into the house without having to walk through it carrying a dirty load?"

Lily nodded, her eyes filling with tears once more. "I'm sorry, ma'am, but I so wanted that guinea. Wiv it I could 'av bought a new dress an' Hannah wouldn't 'av stood a chance. I left the nursery door ajar to show Corby which room an' when 'e asked me to 'old out my hands for my prize he pulled a cord not a coin from 'is pocket and tied them. Then 'e pushed me to the floor and bound me feet, then pulled 'is 'ankie from my pocket and stuffed it into me mouth."

Grace's voice rose in pitch. "Did he give you any clue where he was taking Georgina before he left? Anything? Anything at all?"

Lily shook her head.

George squeezed Grace's hand, not at all sure of the truth of the words he intended to utter but needing to say them anyway. "Steady, my love. We'll find her. He can't have got far."

Lily dabbed her eyes and said miserably, "I'll get my things together, shall I?"

George had never admired Grace more than at that moment when, although filled with maternal panic, she immediately forgave the cause of it. She put her arm around Lily's shoulders and squeezed. "You will not. Plenty more worldy-wise females than you have been taken in by Corbett. The man is a rogue. A hellrake of the first order."

Lily's lip trembled. "You're not turning me off?"

"No, Lily. You may keep your position."

Lily bobbed a very wobbly curtsey. "Thank you, ma'am. I will work ever so 'ard from now on. I prom —" She stopped speaking and frowned. "I remember sommats. He did mutter something when 'e picked up Georgina. It were odd. Turnips. He'd see how the damn baby liked bloody turnips."

It was all George needed to hear. He gave a bark of triumph. "Rouse the household! Search all the root cellars and outhouses in this street and the next one. A lone male carrying a screaming baby — and I will bet all I own Georgina will have been very vocal in her annoyance — would attract the attention of the night watch. Corbett won't have risked taking her far."

Lily jumped to her feet and shot to the door. "An' if I see Corby I'll kick 'im right where it hurts. Twice!"

Grace made to follow her out of the door, but George stayed her with a frown. "The last piece of the puzzle. How the hell did Corbett ever find out we are to be married, let alone the date of the wedding or where it was to be held? Has the man got a crystal ball or something?"

Grace halted and looked back over her shoulder. "Inadvertently, through Jane, I fear. She met with Papa after receiving our invitation. She told him of our plans with realising the import of doing so.. If Papa then mentioned the matter to our stepmother, I think the details would soon have found their way to Corbett."

"Bastard!" George spat. "If he's harmed one hair on Georgina's head, I'll kill him. In fact, when I catch up with him I will be hard-pressed not to do so anyway!"

"You organise the servants into search parties. I'll run and wake Jane and Alfred," Grace said. "Although given Jane's condition, I'll hold back my suspicion that it was she who let the cat out of the bag."

She ran down the stairs and knocked on their bedroom door—thankfully, to find they were both awake and dressed. Alfred sped on his way to join George, leaving Grace to escort Jane downstairs to the parlour. The house was silent no more, with masculine shouts of instructions, doors opening and slamming and the sound of running feet.

Nettie bustled into the parlour with buttered toast and fresh fruit on a tray. "I leave the house for a day to visit my sister and this happens. And it wouldn't have done if I'd been here."

Grace felt faintly nauseous at the sight of food and waved the tray away. Nettie was having none of it. "She won't be found any sooner for you starving yourself, and given her condition, Miss Jane must eat."

Grace gave in and took a slice of toast, and Nettie set the tray down in front of Jane. "Now, Cook said young Tim from the bakery reckons he heard a coach go up the lane to the main road just after midnight. He didn't want to mention it, as he was out setting his traps. Ones that shouldn't have been where he was setting them. Tim kept well out of sight, so he can't say any more than he has."

Grace began to pace as she ate. "I feel so useless. I should be out there with the men. Searching…"

Nettie regarded her and, using the same no-nonsense, 'buck-up, child' tone she had when Grace was young, stated firmly, "When they bring Georgina home — and they will — the first thing she'll want is her mother. You've got to be here. Waiting. Not out and about, goodness knows where."

George entered the room, and Grace looked at him hopefully. "Any news?"

"The staff are visiting each house in the area. It'll make for a quicker search than if Albert and I do it. We'd have to present our card at the front door and wait for a response. Serving staff can go round the back, bang on the kitchen door and state their case straight away. While they get on with it, Albert and I are questioning passers-by in the village and on the outskirts of town. Any news from the search will be bought to us there. Tim from the baker's saw a coach and — "

"I told them that bit," Nettie said.

"But we think it a red herring," George continued. "Mr Palmerston, your nearest neighbour, says a man dressed all in black was carrying a bundle wrapped in something white down the street last night. The moon was full and bright. He's in no doubt of what he saw."

Grace put her hand over her mouth. "Georgina's white shawl is missing."

George nodded grimly. "I know. What worries me though is why wasn't she crying? Woken suddenly and carried from the familiarity of her warm nursery by a stranger? It doesn't make sense."

Grace felt the blood drain from her face. "Lily gave Corbett back the bottle of Glen Eyevie. He's fed drugged whisky to our baby, hasn't he?"

"I fear it."

"Well, he won't have managed to get much of it down her throat," Nanny said stoutly. "A real little madam is our Georgina if you try to put something in her mouth she don't much fancy."

"Enough to make a young babe sleep for a while, though," Jane said. "Let's pray she sets up a screech when she wakes."

There was a shout from outside. George dashed to the window. "Alfred."

George ran to the door. Grace was one step behind him and called over her shoulder, "Stay and take care of Jane, Nettie."

"Hue and cry been sent up at the far end of the street," Alfred told them as they burst out of the front door.

George started to run. Grace picked up her skirts and, uncaring if the neighbours were scandalised by the sight of her lower legs, dashed after him. In the distance her gardener signalled them by waving his arms in the air and shouting, "We've got 'er. We've got 'er, Madam Foston. Round the back in the shed wiv the beets an' the carrots."

Tears of relief poured down Grace's face as without so much as a by your leave she ran through the residence's private garden to see Mrs Barrow, the laundress, cradling Georgina. That lady handed the baby to Grace who took her daughter and planted small kisses all over her face, sobbing as she did so. George put his arm around Grace's shoulders and looked closer. "She is well?"

Georgina opened her eyes, gave them a beatific smile and vomited the sour-smelling contents of her stomach all down the front of her dress. The odour of milk and spirits wafted to Grace's nose. "She is now."

George smiled. Alfred walked to him, tugged his arm and whispered something. Grace couldn't hear what Alfred said but George's smile vanished and she saw a flash of anger in his eyes. "Come, my love. Let me walk you home to Nanny Nettie and Jane. Then Alfred and I have a small matter of business to which we must attend."

"A stranger matching your description of Corbett has been seen in the Dog and Duck this morning according to the butcher, who's just made a delivery up the road," Alfred muttered in George's ear. "A person, the butcher said, who was not quite up to snuff, though he appeared to be trying to be."

"Definitely not up to snuff." George felt the blood boil in his veins as he muttered back, "I'll take Grace home, and we'll go and see if he's still there."

Alfred nodded his agreement and twenty minutes later they set off side by side with matching determined strides. George asked him, "Are you armed, sir?"

Alfred shook his head. "Never thought. Damn. You?"

"No, but it won't stop me wringing the bastard's neck with my bare hands."

A short walk into the outskirts of the town, a left, then a right turn into other residential streets and the inn they sought came into view. They slowed and looked through each of its bottle glass windowpanes. George growled low in his throat when he saw Corbett, standing bold as brass, sipping from a tankard at the bar. Was he so sure his plot had succeeded? Did he not care a child might have died? George's blood froze at that thought.

The bastard deserves to die himself.

"One to each side of him, take an arm apiece, and we'll have him out of there in two shakes of a cat's whisker," Alfred suggested. "Then it's up to you."

George nodded. "I'd like to castrate him on the spot, but I'm sure we can think of some longer and more lingering punishment if we get him out of sight. On the count of three."

They entered the tap room, walked without hurry to the bar and stood to Corbett's left and right. He goggled when he saw George, but before he could react, Alfred twisted his arm up behind his back and they frogmarched him out. Not another soul even blinked when they did, so smoothly and quickly had they nabbed him.

"Let's get him round the back," George said. "Then get out that rusty pocketknife. You debag him and I'll de-ball him."

Corbett went pale, found his voice and spluttered. "You can't... You'll not find the baby if you hurt me. Let me go, and I'll tell you where she is."

"Too late," George growled. "She's back with her mother, and I warned you what would happen if you crossed me again."

Corbett began to struggle, but he was no match for George's muscular frame coupled with Alfred's still battle-ready fitness.

At the rear of the inn was a yard and they took Corbett to the back of it, where a row of fragrant lavender bushes screened the cesspit. George flexed his arm muscles. Hidden from view, Corbett was about to receive his comeuppance.

"It occurs to me..." Alfred said quite conversationally.

The tone of his voice alerted George to glance at his face. From his expression and the ghost of a wink he received, George got the message. While his own thoughts had been clouded by a red mist of anger and he just wanted to beat Corbett to a bloody pulp, Major Winterbottom Retired had been thinking things through. "Yes...?" he replied equally lightly, although it was an effort to do sound in any way carefree.

"Well, you know how it is," Alfred continued, "when a family has a surplus of sons. There's one for the heir, one for the church, one for the army and then, if there is still one left over, one for the navy too. I just happen to have three brothers, you know —"

"You do?"

"Oh, yes. Now, I'm an army man, and in the army we only enlist volunteers. We might take the pipe and drums around the country to encourage the young men to take the King's Shilling, but they still have to make their own mark on the paper, but the navy, now... The navy is a different matter."

George started to get an inkling of where Alfred's thoughts were leading, so went along with the theme. "How so? Do tell."

"The navy are allowed to press men into service. One cosh to the head and any likely prospect not paying attention will wake up seabound for somewhere, say like the Americas, on one of His Majesty's finest frigates. Some men survive the experience and even thrive, most do not, but any that think they'd prefer to jump ship at the next port will be hunted down like dogs and hung from the yardarm."

"You don't say."

"I did mention I had three brothers?"

"The youngest is a jolly jack tar then? Commissioned, I presume?"

Corbett started to struggle once more. "You can't do this. I'm a gentleman, not a bilge rat."

They ignored him.

"Yes. Lieutenant Samuel Winterbottom. Luckily, home on leave. He returns to Devonport shortly."

"How convenient!"

Alfred smiled. "I thought so. No need to go to extremes. I'll hog-tie him and deliver him to my brother. I promise he'll be delighted to receive a new recruit, then neither of us will have this scum's blood on our hands, because I really think the ladies would prefer it."

George didn't hesitate, turned and planted a right-handed uppercut on Corbett's jaw. He swiftly followed it with a left hook to the side of his head just for the heck of it and, after the crunch of bone on bone, blew a satisfied breath over his bruised knuckles as Corbett fell. "I'll fetch rope and transport. You guard him, and we'll get on our way."

Alfred disagreed. "No, my lord. You do the first of the tasks, and *I'll* get on my way. You have an appointment you can't renege on tomorrow. I, on the other hand, will not be so very much missed by the bride if I'm absent."

George grinned and returned in short order with the fastest sports phaeton the nearby livery yard had for hire and the means to bind their prisoner borrowed from the ostler there.

Alfred's knot-tying skills were superb. Corbett was soon immobilized and laid sideways along the footboards below the carriage's seat. Alfred climbed aboard and saluted. "I'll abide at home overnight to rest the pair and, all being well, will be back with you in the morning. Apologise to my wife for my unexpected absence, but having been a military wife for a year or so, Jane was used my disappearing at short notice when I was called in on duty. This is duty of a different kind."

George raised his hand in farewell then returned home at a double-quick half-run.

* * * *

Grace held Georgina tight to her chest as she carried her into the parlour. The baby burbled quite happily to be in her mother's arms now the remaining undigested contents of her stomach had been ejected. She had missed two feeds and would be hungry, and Grace urgently wanted to consult Nettie on the subject.

Jane put her hand to her heart when they walked in. "You found her hale and well?"

Grace nodded, not trusting herself to speak. Her tears had just dried. She would not risk more, even though this time they would be tears of joy.

Nettie jumped to her feet and bustled forward, her face wreathed in smiles. "Praise be! Her colour is good, is it? She is warm, with no tinge of blue on her skin from an overnight chill?"

Grace held her out for Nanny's inspection. "Smelly though."

Nettie reached for the baby. "Give her to me. This little lady needs a bath and a feed. Jane, love, please ring for some tea. Add plenty of sugar to the cup. Grace will still be in shock."

There was no withstanding Nanny when she was at her bossy best, so both complied. Grace sank into a chair, conscious that Nettie was right. She felt weak at the knees and her hands trembled. "I shall try not to be nervous when Georgina is out of my sight for any length of time in the future, I promise. Such a thing will not happen again. George will make sure of it."

Jane rubbed her rounded belly. "As will Alfred. You were the victim of Corbett's spite on this occasion, but I thwarted him as much as you did. It could be my child he picks on next."

Grace agreed a man who would attack a baby in an act of revenge could not be trusted not to do so again, but added a rider. "The man is certainly deranged enough to make another attempt, but George and I will always be at the top of his list for leaving him bare-arsed naked in the middle of a bush."

"You never told me that." Jane bit her lip.

"It was a sight to behold. His bollocks are nothing to be proud of."

Jane spluttered. "Grace, really."

"Really." Grace deliberately chose to misunderstand her sister. "Then we called at the inn and announced we'd just seen a half-naked man, and the crowd set down their tankards and rushed outside. We could hear their laughter for ages as we made our escape on the pony and trap."

Jane's shoulders shook. "Oh, goodness!" She giggled. "What a sight that must have been. How humiliating for him."

"He deserved it, although never in my wildest imaginings did I think Corbett would stoop as low as this."

Jane's laughter burst forth. "He will not do so again."

Grace's spirits lifted as the actuality of her sister's words settled in her mind.

We are safe.

She smiled as the maid set the tea tray before her. The refreshing hot liquid was soon poured and sweetened. Grace picked up her cup and thought she could even fancy a biscuit.

It was more than an hour before George joined them. Jane looked past him then asked, "Alfred?"

"Is escorting His Majesty's newest recruit to the Royal Navy into the custody of Lieutenant Winterbottom, where he can consider himself pressed. Corbett will join his ship at Devonport when Lieutenant Winterbottom returns to active duty shortly."

Grace looked at George's bloodied knuckles. "You assisted him on his way?"

He answered, looking more than pleased with himself, "Of course. You don't lay a hand on my daughter or the love of my life without receiving a sharp reminder from me not to do so again."

Jane looked him direct in the face. "Your daughter?"

He stared her straight in the eye and reiterated, "*My* daughter."

She smiled. "Thank you. I shall not enquire again."

George turned to Grace. "Where is she? She has taken no lasting harm?"

Grace opened her mouth to reply but didn't have to when Nettie walked into the room. "Clean, sweet-smelling and fed. Georgina is now fast asleep in her crib. Lily is watching over her. You, my lord, may see her when she wakes."

Her authority over the nursery reasserted, Nettie relaxed to smile. "Now, away with all of you. You've taken no breakfast to speak of. Cook has laid an early luncheon in the dining room."

George offered each of them an arm. "Come, ladies. Nanny has spoken."

Grace's tummy rumbled and, her appetite restored, she ate a good meal then, while Jane rested on her bed, she and George visited the nursery. An hour later, she left him playing with Georgina, walking his fingers up her belly then tickling under her chin. The tub was being filled in her room. Her longed-for bath had arrived.

A long soak in the hot water with rose-scented soap was bliss. The gown she had selected for her wedding day was hung on the front of her closet door—a lilac-sprigged muslin, it was the prettiest dress she possessed. She surveyed it as she towelled dry.

This time tomorrow we will be husband and wife.

Excited bubbles raced through her middle. An idea formed, and she smiled to herself. An easily removed day dress was her choice to sit down in at dinner, rather than a back-fastening evening gown.

The meal was a quiet affair. She and George refraining from wondering out loud about Alfred's progress in order not to worry Jane, and Jane herself seemed content this was so. Babies and weaning, nursery equipment and staff were the order of the day until Jane yawned. "My apologies. I am starting to feel the weight of the babe I carry these days. I cannot keep my eyes open past ten."

"Of course, you can't." Grace smiled. "Run along. Do you require anything sent up? A milky hot drink, perhaps?"

"Just my bed."

George assisted her sister to rise, and his eyes twinkled as he re-took his seat. "You're not in need of an early night yourself then? I thought you might go with her and leave me to my port."

"I am certainly desirous of my bed, although I have no intention of being the only occupant of it." She stood and lifted the port bottle. "Are you coming?"

He chuckled and picked up their glasses. "Not an offer I'm likely to refuse, my love, even though we are not supposed to see each other the night before we wed, let alone share a bed."

"Pish." She smiled. "Mere superstition. And if the household think it unlucky, they can lump it."

Grace's heart beat faster as they walked up the stairs. She had such a need for George tonight. To be held in his arms, to feel his hardness inside her, and the reassurance of his muscular, warm body pressed against hers. Superstition and scandalized staff be damned, she had decided earlier. Why wait one more lonely, pointless night? George would not be leaving her room. She was going to fall asleep with her cheek on his chest and she was going to wake in the same state come the morning.

George held open her bedroom door for her to precede him. Grace locked it after he followed her in. She offered him the bottle. "Do you care to pour? I swear it is untouched."

He set it down on her dressing table with the glasses. "Later." He sat on a nearby chair and watched Grace pull the pins from her hair, toe off her evening sandals and saunter closer, unfastening the buttons at the side of her dress as she walked. George's eyes never left her. All their lovemaking to date, bar the first afternoon when they had urgently shed their clothing, had taken place when Grace was already undressed and in bed — but this time she intended it to be different. She slipped the loosened gown from her shoulders and shimmied. The dress fell to the floor and pooled around her feet. Lamplight silhouetted her body through the thin silk of her chemise. George's irises darkened. She slipped each small button on the front of the garment through its buttonhole, cupped one breast, her pink nipple hard, and lifted it clear of the garment. "You like?"

"Sweet Jesus... Yes." George's voice was husky with lust as he tugged at his cravat.

Grace pinched the nub of her breast and ran the tip of her tongue over her top lip while gazing provocatively at his groin. "Show me how much."

He undid the front of his britches and freed his erection. Her mouth watered at the sight. "*Mmmm...*"

She pushed her chemise downward to stand before him naked, then stroked her fingers through the golden triangle at the apex of her legs. Oh God. She was wet.

George tugged off his jacket, followed by his shirt and britches, then stood and reached for her.

Grace danced back a step. "Not yet, my lord. To the bed with you. Lay on your back."

She could see his Adam's apple move as he swallowed hard. She waited until he was supine, his beautiful cock standing proud, then swayed toward him and straddled his thighs. She grasped his shaft and teased his cock head through her wet folds. George moaned deep in the back of his throat. "Grace... please..."

She eased his thick manhood inside her channel, her moans joining his as he filled her, then rode his cock harder and faster as her pleasure built. George bucked against the mattress, his head thrown back as his climax arrived. Grace slowed her movements, finding the sweet spot inside her, undulating her hips. Muscles tightened in her belly, spasms pulsed from the mound between her legs, and she cried out the joy of her orgasm. "Yesss..."

Breathing hard, she collapsed onto his chest, and he held her tight until their heart rates slowed, then moved slowly and carefully off his cock and snuggled into his side with one leg draped over his thighs. He put his arm around her and she lifted her face for his kiss, long and deep as their tongues entwined. Her eyelids closed when their lips parted, and Grace fell asleep with the scent of the man she adored in her nose — bergamot — and woke on her wedding day morn to the same.

She pinched George's left buttock. "Up, slug-a-bed. We have an appointment with the vicar, and it will take me longer to get ready than you."

George opened one sleepy eye, leant over and kissed her lips, then put his feet to the floor. "Good morning, sweetheart. We most certainly do."

She watched his manhood disappear inside his britches, his chest inside his shirt, and smiled at the thought they would be naked together later, and all the laters from then on.

George turned back when he reached the door. "I love you, Grace. See you in church."

She gazed into his eyes. "I love you too, George. So very much. See you in church."

Epilogue

Letter from Baron Renfrew to the Earl and Countess of Callander

My friends,

I write to you with such news! You must wish me joy for I am now a married man! I can practically hear your exclamations of surprise at the suddenness of my nuptials, but you have both met my bride, albeit many months ago.

Have you guessed it yet? That her name is Grace? The lady whose hair Cairstine cut and to whom Duncan gifted a set of his boyhood clothes?

Even more, my heart bursts with pride to tell you I now have a sweet little child to call me Papa. Grace and her babe, Georgina, are the loves of my life and I consider myself the most privileged of men to be husband and father to them.

We will visit Corbridge very soon so Grace may select the fabrics and furnishings she desires for Armstrong House, where we intend to reside, along with Back Blindburn. I will hope, once more, to impose on the good nature and hospitality of His Grace, your esteemed parent, Cairstine. Dare I hope to *see you both there? To do so would set the seal on my overflowing happiness.*

Until then, my friends.

Adieu,

George

* * * *

Letter to Baron Renfrew from the Countess of Callander

My dearest friend,

I will confess you guessed entirely right as to our reaction when reading your joyous letter! Such wonderful tidings it brought! We are so delighted for you all. You are a good man, George, and your happiness is well-deserved, especially after the trials and tribulations you've suffered due to your own father's unfortunate condition.

We remember Grace's visit very well. A charming lady of such beauty is not easily forgotten. The attraction between you was palpable and my heart grieved when after your adventure Grace's name was never mentioned again. Until now!

And your sweet daughter's name is Georgina, is it? How mysteriously apt. Be prepared to 'tell all' when we next meet, my friend, for I will not give up until I have wheedled the story of how this came to be from you, and my persistence is legendary!

I know Papa will be delighted to host your visit when you bring Grace and Georgina to Corbridge. Your company is always a pleasure, and speaking of Papa, it is my turn to tease you and leave you wondering now. His Grace has some news of his own, but I will not confide it here, it is his to share. Send me the dates you will be in Corbridge, please?

Until we meet again.

Adieu, adieu,

Cairstine

Want to see more from these authors?
Here's a taster for you to enjoy!

The Scots and the Sassenachs:
The Duke's Lost Love
Raven McAllan & Cassie O'Brien

Coming 2023

Excerpt

Now

By the light of a flaming flambeau held aloft by
Sydney, page and general dogsbody to the Armstrong
household, Mrs. Evanna Percival-Smyth walked home.
The moon was on the wane and that, added to the
heavy cloud obscuring the stars in the night sky, made
his illuminating assistance to guide her footsteps a
necessity. A trip, with its likely consequence of a
twisted ankle, was high on the cards otherwise.

Her house was cloaked in near darkness when she
arrived. No servant would be up waiting. She was not
meant to be there, but rather at Denny House, where
she'd accepted an appointment to chaperone the Lady
Cairstine McColl during her visit to Corbridge.

Circumstances had led to this unexpected return.

Of course, if she chose, she could wake the
household and have people ready to do her bidding

immediately — or almost immediately. It would mean they would have to dress and hurry, probably bleary-eyed or yawning, from their various rooms, and Evanna was more considerate than to ask for that. She valued her staff. Why should her unforeseen homecoming disturb their slumber? In her mind they got little enough respite as it was.

Plus, she had a lot to think about and didn't want anyone to see her agitation. Sydney, bless him, did not count. His intelligence was not of the highest, but he was always willing to please.

At her front door, she opened her reticule and passed her young escort a silver sixpence. His eyes widened.

"Cor, Mrs P. Thank you."

She patted his shoulder and smiled, even though with her knees all atremble after seeing Cairstine's father, Nathan, for the first time in twenty years it was the last thing she felt like doing. She wanted to run and hide. Be alone.

Think things over.

Sydney stared at her, a slight frown creasing between his eyebrows. "You all right, Mrs. P? You looked a bit strange just then."

Bless him. "You're a good lad, Sydney. I'm fine, just tired, I suspect. Run along now. I imagine there will be plenty for you to do tomorrow. Is your bed ready?"

He nodded. "Course it is. I's been mekking it tidy every morning like what you told me to."

"Good boy. Take the flambeau to guide you but be sure to extinguish it in the water bucket when you get home."

He nodded and dashed off.

Evanna watched him disappear and reached into her reticule, which along with a quantity of small change, also contained her door key. She let herself in and sighed in satisfaction at the familiar scent of her own home—lavender and beeswax. Her housemaid had obviously not skimped on either the elbow grease or the furniture polish while she'd been away. An oil lamp, its wick turned down low, lit the interior and saved her fumbling about in the dark. It took but a second to pluck it from a small consul table and make her way up the stairs to her boudoir. By the lamp's absence her servants would know she had returned.

Her thoughts were all over the place as she mulled over the events of the evening just gone. A large sherry to calm her agitation was in order, she decided. Once it was poured, Evanna settled back into her chair and thought back to when it had all started. Her first and only visit to Edinburgh…

* * * *

Before

The excitement began when she'd overheard her father's dour tones followed by her mother's firm but snappish retort from the other side of a not-quite-closed door.

"It would cost a small fortune! I'm nae made o' money for you to fritter away on female foibles and frolicking, woman."

"It's got nothing to do with frolicking or frittering, Angus Kerr," her mama retorted with a hard edge to her voice that Evanna had never heard her employ when addressing Papa before. Forceful. That was it. Intrigued, she continued to listen.

"Evanna is the prettiest of our girls as well as the eldest. Just give me five hundred pounds to take her to Edinburgh…"

Evanna held her breath, hardly daring to hope.

"And I'll practically guarantee she'll catch herself a well-to-do husband. Then she can sponsor each of her younger sisters when they are of marriageable age. That's four for the price of one. Consider it an investment. After all, it's not much more than you spent on that gelding last month."

Her father fired back, "At least the gelding crossed the finishing line first and brought home the prize fund."

"An aberration, no doubt." Her mother sounded less than impressed. "Let's face it, it's about time one of your stable achieved a positive result. Your racehorses cost more than all of we females do put together. The gelding's winnings should meet the majority of the expenses I'll incur in Edinburgh."

"But…but…five hundred pounds," her father said glumly.

"You think on my words, Angus. You fathered them and you have a responsibility to see your daughters respectably established."

The rustling of stiffened petticoats warned Evanna it was time to move. She picked up her skirts and hurried away.

Would she get to Edinburgh?

* * * *

Now

Nathaniel, Duke of Glenard sank gratefully into the padded comfort of a fireside chair and accepted the balloon glass of brandy offered to him by his daughter, Cairstine. The concern in her eyes mirrored the tone of her voice as he took his first sip. "You look quite knocked up, Papa. Drink this and we'll talk in the morning. There's no rush now the letter has been destroyed."

Knocked up, knocked sideways and thoroughly knocked off kilter. Nathan could only manage a nod. One image filled his mind to the exclusion of all else. There was no room for more.

Evanna… My love…

Cairstine smiled softly and walked to the door. If she was disappointed at his lack of response in not enquiring as to her own part in the affair of the treasonable letter that had brought them all hotfoot to Corbridge, she didn't show it. He would make it up to her in the morning. Ask all manner of questions about her adventures over the last few weeks. Tell of his own and express his happiness at her marrying the very man he would have chosen for her if she had not already done so herself — Duncan, the Earl of Callander. But for tonight he needed some time alone with his thoughts.

Evanna…

* * * *

Before

He first saw her at an evening entertainment he attended at the Assembly Rooms in Edinburgh. His father had decided his twenty-year-old heir required a little Town polish before his introduction to the height of the Ton during the official London Season the following year, so had dispatched him to the Scottish capital to reside with his Godfather Sir Douglas Wallace to experience the festivities enjoyed by the minor nobility and wealthy gentry who resided in the city. Sir Douglas' own son, Alain, although older, was not so far above Nathan in age as for them to have little in common, and their friendship had been cemented one evening while downing an after-dinner bottle of port.

Alain winked when the dining room door swung shut behind Sir Douglas. His wife, Alain's mother, had long since retired to bed. "I fancy another round. How about you?"

Nathan, enjoying the mellow feeling imbibing the wine induced, agreed. A fresh bottle was soon delivered by way of the butler and, once uncorked, Alain dismissed the servant with a lazy wave of his hand. "We'll see ourselves up, thank you."

Nathan sipped and found the flavor as richly satisfying as he had the contents of the previous bottle.

"So…" Alain said. "How did you find the ladies sauntering in the park this afternoon? Did any of them catch you eye? I thought Lady Merrythorpe was looking rather hopefully in your direction. She's recently *enceinte* and free to follow her own inclinations for the next couple of months, you know?"

Nathan cheeks heated to his hesitant reply. "Ah… She is…? Um…?"

Alain hooted with laughter. "You never have, have you? Come along. Admit it. You're still as pure as the driven snow."

Nathan fidgeted uncomfortably in his seat at the truth of that particular statement. An edition of engraved prints that included Ruben's famous nudes of Venus, Angelica and Andromeda were his sole education on how men differed from women beneath their clothes. Apart from one stolen kiss under the mistletoe the previous Christmas, the book, his imagination and his right hand were indeed his total experience of the fairer sex to date. "Well…not exactly."

Alain eyed him knowingly. "So, what did you get? A kiss or two? Or maybe she let you slip your hand down her bodice and feel her breast?"

That the kiss had been the extent of it Nathan chose not to admit, so instead he nodded.

Alain grinned. "Well, that's a situation we must rectify as soon as may be. A young matron up for some fun times will at the very least expect you to know what goes where and when. Gird your loins, my friend. You and I are going pay a call at Mother MacDonald's fine establishment tomorrow evening."

Nathan swallowed hard as nerves and mounting excitement at the prospect played their part. "We are?"

Alain tossed down the remaining port in his glass. "Be careful how much wine you take with dinner. The proprietress of the house we shall visit after it will not permit admittance to any gentleman she suspects of being too tipsy to treat her valuable merchandise with care."

Nathan set his unfinished wine down on the table and drank no more before they retired to bed. If he was to further his education with regards to the fairer sex, he'd best be on fine form come the morrow.

* * * *

It took two whole days fidgeting with tense expectation every time her mother entered the room before an announcement was finally made. The family was indeed decamping to Edinburgh for a visit to last several weeks.

Evanna was sat reading whilst her younger sisters concentrated on setting stitches into their samplers in one of the least gloomy rooms in Kerr Castle, designated by their mother as the 'ladies parlor' — although the term parlor did rather flatter what had previously been a guardhouse in which the tall, open arrow slits had been glazed.

Her mother entered the room and clapped her hands to garner their attention. "Girls. Your father and I have come to a decision. A house has been rented. We are removing to the capital next week."

Evanna closed her book, her tummy full of excitable wriggling worms while her sisters sat straighter and with their eyes shining, exclaimed. "Oh, Mama. We are? How wonderful…"

Lady Kerr regarded their faces wreathed in smiles and frowned. "We are and I expect you younger girls to be of use to Evanna when necessary. To walk in the park with her or accompany her on any other daytime activity where it would be unseemly for your sister to be alone. I myself will chaperone her to any evening parties, of course."

Evanna's stomach lurched guiltily as her sisters' smiles faded.

"We are not to attend the evening parties?"

"We are to be left behind?"

"That's not fair…"

"Fair has nothing to do with it," Lady Kerr stated firmly. "Evanna is the eldest and you younger girls must wait your turn. If she does well and makes a good match, she will be in a position to aid you both, but for her to do so, you need to return the favor."

Oh, goodness! I don't much like the sound of that. What happens if I don't?

Evanna smiled nervously at her siblings and promised. "I will do my best."

"Of course, you will," her mama said briskly. "Now, come with me. Our budget is not endless and Great Grandma's trunk awaits. Given the fuller skirts she wore I can think of at least two dresses that when unpicked will supply enough material to fashion an evening cape and a shawl. You younger girls can have the stitching of them while Evanna reads out loud."

At this pronouncement Evanna felt ten times worse. Not only were her sisters to be denied the pleasure of music and dancing, but to rub salt into the wound, as her own skill with a needle was abysmal, they had the tedious job of sewing garments they would not wear for parties they would not attend. She would make it up to them, she decided. Do her best to attract attention of a suitable beau who would be rich and handsome and good-natured enough to welcome his wife's siblings whensoever they chose to visit.

He will have to, for I will accept nothing less.

* * * *

Nathan found he could barely concentrate on his dinner with thoughts of what was to come after. It was with relief that he set his glass on the table when Alain stood and excused them both to his father after only one circuit of the port bottle.

If he had tried to drink any more it would probably have choked him. Nerves were uppermost as he dwelled on what was to come. What if he couldn't perform? Was laughed at? Gossiped about? It was not a scenario to be born.

Common sense told him also it was not likely to happen. As Alain had explained earlier, the ladies knew what to do and enjoyed showing a virgin how to go about things.

There would not be any problems. He would, as they said, get it up, get it in and get on with it.

The evening was remarkably fine with a full moon to light their way as they walked along Canongate. Alain paused before a house that looked no different from its tall, grey residential neighbors then pulled a black velvet opera mask from his pocket and handed it to Nathan. "You may remove it when you are private with your choice of female if you wish, but within the public room, guests remain discreetly masked."

Nathan's hand shook a little as he tied the strings at the back of his head and smoothed the soft material over his nose and the center of his face. Using his ebony walking cane, Alain rapped on the door. Three sharp taps, followed by a gap of a few seconds, then two more. It swung open and a liveried footman bowed them into a lavishly decorated vestibule stylized in a theme of an Ancient Greek or Roman temple. Colonnaded stone pillars supported a vaulted ceiling and on the walls in between them beautifully embroidered tapestries depicted the naked frolicking of gods and goddesses that normally filled Nathan's wet dreams. A stone altar fulfilled the role of a desk and behind it, beautifully coiffured and gowned, sat a woman in her middle years.

She looked up as they entered and smiled. "Good evening, gentlemen, and welcome. You have pre-purchased invitations?"

Alain produced two gilt-edged cards with a flourish and handed them over. "Of course, madam."

She surveyed them with satisfaction. "Our gold service, I see. Very good. Please proceed to the inner sanctum and enjoy all the delights our temple of love has to offer."

Nathan followed Alain through the door she indicated and tried not to gape at the females scantily clad in near-translucent white Grecian robes, lounging on various sofas ranged around the salon. Some were in the company of a gentleman, like himself and Alain, masked, while others sat alone looked up with languid interest at the new arrivals. As in the vestibule, the room was lit by glass-shaded lanterns burning sweet-smelling oil, and a far older lady, more modestly clothed, added to the ambiance by way of producing tinkling notes from a pianoforte.

One couple rose from a chaise, the gentleman displaying a visibly enlarged bulge at the front of his breeches. His female companion took his hand and led him from the room. A servant approached with filled wine glasses set on a silver tray. Nathan waited to follow Alain's lead as to whether he should accept one.

Alain did so, and once Nathan had taken his own Alain told him in a low undertone, "Madame believes a glass or two enhances the experience, but those who wish to imbibe more would be better entertained in a drinking den rather than her salon. Come. Let's take a casual amble around the room and find a goddess that tickles your fancy?"

Nathan swallowed hard and tried not to stare at the quantity of exposed flesh on offer. Alain reassured him, "You will find no false pretense here as to the purpose of this house. It is perfectly acceptable to direct your gaze towards the feminine attributes that attract you. No person in this room is unwilling or bashful. It's the secret of Madame's success. The goddesses take enjoyment in the manner in which they earn their bread."

Feeling more relaxed with this knowledge, Nathan looked around him with interest and found his eyes drawn to the voluptuous curves of a raven-haired female. Excitement shivered down his spine. Her breasts were mouth-wateringly luscious. They could be in his hands shortly should he wish, and his groin was telling him he very much did. He nudged Alain's arm and indicated his preference.

Alain nodded sagely. "The goddess Celeste. A good choice. I've lain with her several times. She's an experienced lover who certainly knows how to please a man. I'll walk over with you. Personally, I'm hoping the naughty little minx known as Luna is in the temple tonight. She emptied my balls three times the last time I visited."

Three times? Oh, yes, please…

That his entrance ticket allowed for more than just one encounter was thrilling, and Nathan walked forward with a spring in his step. Alain bowed when they reached the lady in question. "Good evening, Celeste. May I introduce my *young* friend? Lord N is desirous of spending some time in your company?"

With a soft smile, Celeste nodded, and Nathan sensed a coded message had been sent and understood. She patted the cushioned seat beside her. "A delightful honor. Come sit beside me, my lord. Let us sit and share a glass of wine while we confide our desires."

Nathan did so and Alain walked away. Celeste beckoned a servant and once each of them had taken a freshly filled glass she looked into his eyes. "I believe you are nervous, my lord. Will you confess it? Have I the privilege of being your first coupling?"

Nathan nodded dumbly. She leant forward, took his glass and set it down. Her breasts brushed against his chest. "I believe you would like to be private with me rather than dally in this salon?"

"Yes..."

She held out her hand. "Then our bed of pleasure awaits."

Celeste led him through an arch then up the stairs and into a corridor that had a series of closed doors along its length. A lit lantern stood on the floor outside some, but not all. She picked one up, opened the door and proceeded him in. "The light signals the room is unoccupied and prepared for our use."

Nathan surveyed the room's contents, which at first glance resembled those of a boudoir, but on closer inspection contained items more unusual to find in a bedchamber than the draped bed standing at its center. A sturdy padded stool, higher than looked comfortable to sit or perch upon, had turned wood finials jutting out at right angles on its legs. On top of the washstand were glass bottles containing an oily liquid, and beside them were what appeared to be wickless candles, phallic in shape, along with a housemaid's feather duster and a pair of velvet mittens.

He began to imagine the ways in which these items could be employed, but not for long. Celeste, with a knowing half-smile, unclasped the golden belt at her waist. The silky, diaphanous material of her robe slithered from her shoulders and pooled on the floor at her feet.

Nathan stared. He couldn't help it. No still life, no matter how artfully painted, could portray the soft, sumptuous curves of nakedness now displayed to his gaze. His hands ached to touch and his balls tightened, demanding release.

With a sway of her hips, Celeste walked to the bed and lay down on it. "Would you care to disrobe and join me, my lord?"

Never before had Nathan shed his clothing at such a pace. Without a care for creases, his garments were soon in a heap on the floor, his bashfulness vanishing as desire to spill his seed inside this goddess increased. His manhood sprang to attention and Celeste encouraged him to come closer while stroking her fingers between her legs.

"That's it, my lord. See, my secret place is ready and awaiting your pleasure…"

Nathan needed no second urging. Celeste parted her legs as he lay over her and guided his pre-cum-coated cock to where it most wanted to be. The sensation was beyond anything his wet dreams had provided. Warm, smooth and all-encompassing feminine softness surrounded his shaft. He let out a small moan. She lifted her hips to his and he thrust inside her—one, twice, three times—then his climax exploded. With a groan he stilled and mumbled softly. "Ah… Sorry, I…"

She shushed him and kissed his neck. "There now. For a first time I would have been more surprised if it wasn't so. But you're a young man. The urge will be back with you before many minutes have passed, then we can make love again in a more leisurely manner."

Less than half an hour later, Nathan was delighted to find her words came true. The intervening time was spent exploring Celeste's naked curves as she instructed him which touches enhanced her pleasure. He learnt where her sensitive nub was hidden, how to fondle it tenderly while her excitement, and his, built. When he mounted her again, he was more aware of the lover beneath him and could match his thrusts to her urging rather than being wrapped up in only his own.

His second climax arrived with a shout of ecstasy, and as Celeste mewled beneath him breathing heavily, he hoped he had satisfied her too.

He disengaged and moved to one side. She turned towards him and held him close. He didn't mean to, but secure in her arms with his cheek resting on one plump breast and his hand cupping the other, he fell into a blissful sleep. It was daylight when he awoke. Celeste patted his bare buttock.

"Up with you, my lord. All guests must depart come the dawn."

Nathan smiled a little sheepishly. "Thank you. It was a wonderful night."

Celeste stood, picked up her robe and blew him a kiss. "Then come and see us again soon."

"You can be sure I will," he murmured as she left the room.

He re-dressed and found Alain waiting for him when he entered the vestibule. Alain winked. "There you are. About time. I don't know about you, but all this activity has left me ravenous for breakfast."

Nathan agreed, but the temple held one more surprise for him as they departed, when a masked lady wearing an evening dress of the finest quality entered the vestibule from the direction of the private rooms in the company of a masked gentleman. Nathan nudged Alain's arm. He looked, shrugged, and said in an undertone, "If a couple not wed to each other require a little discreet privacy in which to conduct their affair, they may purchase a silver boudoir ticket from Madam. With such, ladies are welcome here, so long as they stay within the boundaries of the rules like the gentlemen."

Nathan tried for an air of nonchalance at this unexpected turn of events. "Ah, well, yes. I suppose so."

Lord, I've got a lot to learn. I've got to come back as soon as I can. Tonight? Hmm…yes…tonight for sure.

He found himself distracted for the rest of the day — his thoughts consumed by the lovemaking he'd enjoyed and of future delights yet to come. He returned to the temple that evening, and the next, and the next several after that. He enjoyed Celeste's company once more, along with that of Venus and Diana, and the contents of the washstand were no longer a mystery for him. It was like an addiction he couldn't get enough of — until the day when he opened his money pouch to take out the coins required to purchase his entrance ticket and it felt somewhat light.

Nathan counted the golden guineas remaining and swallowed hard. More than half of the funds handed to him by his father to cover his expenses while in Edinburgh were gone — and they had been more than generous. He would not ask for more. He didn't regret the manner in which his coins had been spent. How could he when they had made a man of him? But there would be no more expensive visits to the temple, he decided. On the wall, a framed pen-and-ink sketch of Edinburgh Castle caught his eye. He picked up his hat and gloves and set out to view the castle in person.

About the Authors

Raven McAllan

After 30 plus years in Scotland, Raven now lives near the east Yorkshire coast, with her long-suffering husband, who is used to rescuing the dinner, when she gets immersed in her writing, keeping her coffee pot warm and making sure the wine is chilled.

With a new home to decorate and a garden to plan, she's never short of things to do, but writing is always at the top of her list.

Her other hobbies include walking along the coast and spotting the wildlife, reading, researching, cros stitch and trying not to drop stitches as she endeavours to knit.

Being left-handed, and knitting right-handed, that's not always easy.

Cassie O'Brien

I love:

Being with family and friends.

Writing and having the freedom to do so now child four of four has passed her driving test and is off to uni later this year.

I Like:

Any excuse to throw a party.

Any excuse to open a bottle of fizz.

Shoes in vast quantities – the higher the heel the better.

Ambitions:

To write many more books.

To own a pair of Louboutin's.

To never go near an iron or a hoover again.

Raven and Cassie love to hear from readers. You can find their contact information, website details and author profile page at https://www.totallybound.com

Home of Erotic Romance

Sign up for our newsletter and find out about all our romance book releases, eBook sales and promotions, sneak peeks and FREE romance books!

www.ingramcontent.com/pod-product-compliance
Lightning Source LLC
Chambersburg PA
CBHW051824170626
46807CB00003B/1011